Praise for Eden Winter's shifters:

A Bear Walks into a Bar (2016 Rainbow Awards Honorable Mention)

This book was incredible! While maintaining some common shifter lore aspects, this book took on a whole new twist to a stale genre.

~Elisa Rolle

I loved everything about this book. All of the characters are fantastic, although I'll admit to a little preference for the oh-so-adorable Brad, the fox shifter with the libido from hell and the cutest personality ever! Seriously, my friends, don't miss out on this. It's hot, beyond hot, fun, and made me feel good. What else can you ask for?

~Christy Duke

Naked Tails

This is a book to savor - every word, every page. It is definitely a character-driven book, and what characters they are! NAKED TAILS is like an addictive drug.

~Mrs. Condit and Friends

And P.D. Singer's shifters:

Otter Chaos (with Tail Slide)

Unusual but beautiful - I've never felt that much under-standing with a wild animal. Not to mention that some of Lon's shenanigans were roll-on-the-floor funny. It's been a while since I earned a "shhh" for laughing too hard.

~Feliz Faber

Other titles by Eden Winters:

The Diversion Novels
Diversion (Diversion #1)
Collusion (Diverion #2)
Corruption (Diversion #3)
Manipulation (Diversion #4)
Redemption (Diversion #5)

Other Novels
A Matter of When
The Angel of Thirteenth Street
Fallen Angel
Settling the Score
The Telling
The Wish
Duet
Naked Tails
A Bears Walks Into a Bar

Other Titles from P.D. Singer

The Mountain Novels
Fire on the Mountain
Snow on the Mountain
Fall Down the Mountain
Blood on the Mountain
Return to the Mountain

Other Novels
The Rare Event
A New Man
Spokes
Otter Chaos
Diving Deep

From Eden:

Many thanks to P.D. Singer, who is always an inspiration, an awesome collaborator, a wonderful friend, and without whom I'd never have made the leap to published author.

From P.D.:

Thanks to Eden Winters for creating characters I had to play with, TD O'Malley for encouragement and butt-kicks, and Angela Benedetti, for not laughing. Much.

Warning: this book contains graphic depictions of male/male sex, and is not intended for audiences under the age of eighteen. This book is a work of fiction. All characters, companies, events, and locations are either products of the author's imagination or are used fictitiously. Any resemblance to actual persons, living or dead, places, or events is entirely coincidental and beyond the intent of the author and publisher.

Two Bears and a Baby
Copyright © Eden Winters and P.D. Singer 2017
Cover art by Jacqueline Sweet
Layout and design by P.D. Singer

ISBN: 978-1-62622-041-6

Published by:
Rocky Ridge Books
PO Box 6922
Broomfield, CO 80021
http://RockyRidgeBooks.com

two

BEARS

and a
Baby

EDEN WINTERS
P.D. SINGER

ROCKY RIDGE BOOKS

CHAPTER ONE

Keep your friends close and your enemies closer. Sawyer Ballantine didn't like having either close this early in the morning. Not when they were likely to bring down the doe grazing peacefully in the snow-free patch outside his cabin door.

Stone-gray shapes drifted between the pines—they'd scented breakfast on the hoof. Six, no, seven wolves... Maybe they'd inhale enough there wouldn't be more than a scrap of shinbone and a rib left once they'd eaten. Not like the mess they left last time.

Sawyer rumbled deep in his throat. The wolves didn't get to bring their business to his doorstep. The Urso of Ballantine Mountain deserved more respect. Even if they brought an entire haunch as tribute, they didn't get to hunt on his private grounds.

He slapped the window with one broad hand. The doe jerked her head up and dashed, not even stopping to flare her nostrils. She hadn't been alert enough to notice the danger creeping up on her but made up for the lack now, bolting at the thud of his palm on the glass.

Sawyer stepped through the slider, heedless of the chill mountain air on his bare chest and feet. He hadn't troubled to pull on more than jeans after a night in the sack with his lover. Let the wolves get a look at his bulk, all six foot two and two hundred and twenty pounds as a man. Remind them he could be seven hundred pounds of grizzly rage chasing them at thirty-five miles per hour.

"Get over here!" Sawyer bellowed. He'd built the cabin sturdily enough Dillon might sleep through the summons, and much as he wanted to get his Arth in on this confrontation, he didn't have the luxury of time to go wake him. Dillon was still learning the fine art of managing a mountain full of shifters. The mangy mongrels creeping through his woods heard Sawyer clearly enough.

One wolf bolted after the doe but hadn't pursued her far. He stopped at the base of the deck. Lolling his drippy tongue at Sawyer, he paused a moment, letting the rest of his pack join him.

Seven wolves gathered and rippled back into two-footed pains in the ass. Two women, five men, all naked as jay birds, and not a one of them doing a thing to disguise it. Hmm, Margo the nurse, TJ the electrician, Carl the truck driver, a couple of his drywall crew, Josh from excavations, Lilly the... who cared, she was hunting on his grounds.

"You rang?" their leader drawled.

Brian. Insolent pup, of course he'd be the instigator. Rudy hadn't crushed the upstart yet. What was he waiting for? Sawyer's former second-in-command wouldn't remain Lobo long if he didn't get his fuzzy tail in gear and deal with the biggest threat to his leadership.

"Did I give you leave to hunt my land?" Sawyer growled.

"The deer don't care if it's your land," Brian shot back. "And neither do we."

"This is Ballantine Mountain and you should care."

No one ever thought a bear could move as fast as Sawyer could. In a heartbeat he'd dropped from the deck to the ground before the wolves, and had Brian by the scruff of the neck. Bastard thought he could be the alpha? Let him deal with the fallout from their impudence.

"My woods. My game. Any bloody mess near the house, my bloody mess." Sawyer shook his handful. So tempting to break him, right here and now. "Could be you if you keep mouthing off."

One of Brian's companions whined in the back of his throat, but not Brian. Idiot. He could be dead before his cronies could shift and intervene.

"Yeah, yeah, fighting your pal Rudy's battles for him again." Brian spoke with a twist of pain in his voice to mark the massive hand halfway squeezing his spine to pulp. It would be child's play to shift that hand completely, let the claws finish off the troublemaker... And do exactly what Brian accused him of.

Damn it all, why hadn't Rudy dealt with his challenger by now? Sawyer spared a curse for the Lobo.

"Fighting my own, pup. Bring down prey on my doorstep, would you? I'll take the whole kill if you do." Venison would be right tasty, too. Winter was nearly over, the fierce hungers of hibernation time waning, but a slab of deer steak tossed at the grill never came amiss.

"Big bad bear is a thief?" The fool in his clutches trusted entirely too much to Sawyer's good nature.

"I am master here, dog." He shook Brian again, harder. So easy to snap his neck... So tempting. The others stepped back—Sawyer manhandled the strongest of them. If they rushed as a group, things would get a little busy. And bloody.

Nothing Sawyer couldn't heal with a shift or two, but then he was back to a bloody mess outside his winter home. "And you will remember it."

He forced the wolf to bend before him, his massive strength enough to bend his challenger even without the weight of his bear-self.

"You going to pound my ass like you pound that pussy Rudy's?" Would this damn dog never learn? Sawyer'd taken Rudy often enough, hard not to smell it on him. Not that scent markings were easy to smell beyond Eric, the Wapiti of the local elk herd, but there'd been more to their joinings than domination.

"Think I should?" Sawyer rumbled. Maybe he should stick his dick into the wolf just to teach him manners. Wouldn't be the first shifter he'd schooled, but not like this. Not with Dillon upstairs. His mate. His bear lover, and his companion. Sawyer wouldn't do anyone without Dillon's participation and cooperation, and he had other ways of making a point. With one massive mitt he forced the wolf to bow before him. "Better bend over."

A gasp came out of the pack, and someone was brave enough to snarl, though Sawyer quieted that nonsense with a growl of his own.

"Think your ass is ready?"

A thin whimper came from the wolf in his grasp, and the stink of fear. Good.

Sawyer smacked the flat of his free hand against the rounded humps of rump before him. Again he struck, and again, forcing yips of shock from his victim. Hard enough to sting his palm, more than hard enough to make his point. A fourth slap against Brian's butt ought to drive the lesson home. He landed the blow and thrust the wolf away, letting him stumble and nearly fall into the pine duff.

"I am Sawyer Ballantine. This is my mountain. You do not hunt on my doorstep. Now get your furry asses out of here."

Seven gray forms hit the forest floor with four feet and raced away, tails down but not all of them tucked.

The Lobo better bring this bunch to heel before he stopped being Lobo. Sawyer couldn't fight Rudy's battles for him.

CHAPTER TWO

The doe went one way, the wolves another. Satisfied, Sawyer rubbed his tingling palm and stepped back into the comfort of his cabin. Some cabin—the outside might be huge, squared-off logs, but the inside offered comfort to rival any of the swanky houses back in town.

Sawyer took all he'd learned creating luxury condominiums and employed the best materials and features into his home.

The high ceiling peaked into the roof with no worries for the tons of snow it supported, and flames crackled in a fireplace big enough to roast the entire ox he'd jested about being hungry for.... Last week. He'd settle for the deer this morning.

Hibernation time must be drawing to a close. Hard enough to keep a business running when he needed a third of the year to eat, sleep, and fuck for sixteen hours a day.

A heavy sleep-sigh gusted from the open bedroom door. Dillon hadn't wakened. Much as Sawyer needed to teach the only other bear in his sleuth how to be a proper bear, Dillon needed the sleep. Natural remedy for what ailed him. Or better be. Sawyer slid out of his jeans and back into bed. Risking the chill of his skin waking his toasty-warm, maybe even too warm, lover, Sawyer snugged up to Dillon's back.

How had he survived last year's hibernation? Alone, when his few waking hours needed the touch and company of another bear? Not just any bear had come into his life, but Dillon, strong, young, handsome. And gay as Sawyer. He could have sent in a custom order for a mate and not gotten anyone as perfect as Dillon. Then again, he also might not have gotten the rest of the motley crew he'd plucked out of a bar in a wide-spot-on-the-road mountain town. Three other young shifters not welcome in their home packs or skulks, all trying to make a living and take care of each other. His Dillon had looked after Jerry and Kevin and Brad, and they him, and now Sawyer had the lot of them.

A solid unit. Loyal to a fault.

Not that he wanted quite as many of the merry ménage as currently occupied the bed. At least at the moment.

Brad rolled over, his black paws waving in the air. His bushy tail stuck out behind when he uncurled, sending the red brush of fur into Dillon's face.

Dillon sneezed explosively, jerking back and nearly flattening Sawyer's nose.

"That's enough, Brat!" Sawyer swiped the surprised fox up and dropped him over the edge of the bed. "Go find Kevin."

Shouldn't be hard: if Sawyer wanted either of the wolves, he'd go look in one of the other four bedrooms, the one with the whiff of semen. Why Brad had ambled in here last night wasn't too clear, but having the little guy in the bed didn't crowd the bears any. Once he fell asleep, he shifted and cuddled. And sometimes got rolled over on.

Brad lolled his tongue out from the doorway and trotted away. Leaving Dillon to rub the tickle out of his nose also left him alone for Sawyer's bare hugs.

They hardly had any time alone these days, what with the wolves, foxes, the occasional elk, a random possum who showed up to court their bobcat housekeeper, the brave fellow, and at least half of them ending up in the bed. But now, just him and Dillon.

Sawyer wrapped thick, muscular arms around Dillon from behind. Pulling him back meant moving a grown man nearly as large as himself, but didn't hurt to remind him of Sawyer's strength. None of their menagerie could match either of them, but Dillon couldn't match Sawyer now, and maybe never would, potential alpha though he was. He'd grown into those shoulders this winter, filling out with their housekeeper's excellent cooking, the occasional elk (nobody who shifted) and heh, a steady diet of semen. Perfect spice for their lives.

Dillon and his pals were insatiable, with all the horniness of the early twenties male plus the natural randiness of their species. Almost made Sawyer feel old. For about twelve seconds, until the hibernation lust hit again. Like now.

"Awake now?" Sawyer nuzzled into Dillon's ear. "Or should I say, are you up now?"

"Oh yeah." Dillon reached back to haul Sawyer's hips closer to his ass. That delectable, tight ass, still a little slick from last night.

"I'm up too," was both obvious and true. Just getting close to Dillon put the lead in Sawyer's pencil, which was a lot closer to a log. And in just the right place to rub into his lover's crack. That and a friendly reach around made a dandy "good morning."

Oh Moon, but Sawyer loved his bear. Maybe Dillon was the only other bear on his mountain, but hardly a consolation prize. No wonder he'd been thrown out of his old sleuth, with his aura of power and taste for cock.

What made him unacceptable to the bears of the Black Hills Sleuth made him perfect for Sawyer.

Dillon was awake all right, pushing back and rocking for all he was worth. Sawyer growled his pleasure into his lover's neck, loving the rasp of whiskers against skin and the travel of rod against crack. Oh hell yes, but... was he..?

Yes, he was still lubed enough, more than eager enough. Sawyer pulled back to aim. Dillon welcomed him in.

The tight passage of his bear-honey's ass made a fine, fine place to be. Might be cold outside but it was hot enough to melt him in here. Holding on tighter and flicking a nipple, Sawyer groaned at the perfection of welcoming his lover to spring and a new season.

The muscular solidity of the man he held drove Sawyer to greater effort. Steering with a big handful of Sawyer's butt, Dillon aimed him just so, right at the sweet spot. His moans were the best music, his gasps a reward. With a handful of stiff cock, Sawyer pleasured his lover from both directions until Dillon pulsed and cried out something so deep and primal Sawyer could have drowned in the wordless praise. He joined his mate in the throes of orgasm. Spurting his seed deep into Dillon's body, Sawyer could only hold on tightly and ride the crest of climax.

They collapsed into a puddle of satisfied bear. He'd withdraw, but he wouldn't let go. No, Sawyer'd never let go. He didn't want to, he didn't have to, and in some ways, he couldn't, even if he wanted to. Why would he? They'd bonded deeply at the beginning of the year's cold, and now, when the first bulbs forced green shoots through the snows, they'd learned some small measure of what their bonding meant.

Sawyer nuzzled into the curls grown long at the back of Dillon's neck. "Good morning. Happy spring."

A deep chuckle shook Dillon's sturdy frame. "Happy spring to you." He patted the cheek he'd been steering with and rolled to snuggle against the pelt on Sawyer's chest. Even on a king bed, his feet stuck over the edge, making a tent of the goose down comforter.

Happy wasn't enough to describe this spring. Sawyer rubbed his cheek against the top of Dillon's head. There might be only two bears in the sleuth of Ballantine Mountain, but enough love to fill every vale and hollow.

Their peace didn't last long—Dillon shot out of bed, running for the bathroom. Definitely green around the gills.

CHAPTER THREE

Torn between going to hold Dillon's head and letting the guy heuk it out in peace, Sawyer opted to pretend he wasn't hearing the gagging coming from the bathroom. His own gorge rose at the sound. What exactly had they eaten?

Their housekeeper, Liza, surely hadn't served anything likely to cause a problem, had she? For last night's dinner she'd prepared trout, two big brookies apiece, and fresh from the stream. One of the otters brought tribute.

Did the otters hold a grudge? Nope, didn't fit anything Sawyer knew about them. Playful and peaceful, unless they were defending their young. Sawyer had less trouble from them than of anyone else on Ballantine Mountain. He'd resolved most of the trouble with the elk. Once he'd let Dillon have a little heart to heart with the herd's Wapiti, they'd all learned something, not least of all that Dillon made a perfect match for the Urso he owed fealty to.

Nope, the potatoes shouldn't have been a problem, even swimming in sweet butter, and broccoli almost tasted good with cheese sauce—was that the source of Dillon's stomach ailment? Dratted Liza kept trying to "feed the omnivores some healthy green stuff." Sawyer didn't mind a little sedge or biscuit-root while shifted, but fluffy biscuits and honey went down better.

13

And apparently came up, too. Sawyer's belly flipped in sympathy with the retching from the other room.

Eventually Dillon returned, his eyes red-rimmed from the ordeal. He smelled of spearmint and soap. Now only Sawyer smelled like they'd had sex three times in twelve hours. A good smell. The best.

Only, not at the moment, to Dillon. Halfway back into bed, his nostrils flared. Instead of sinking into Sawyer's outstretched arms, he pelted back into the bathroom.

Armpit check. One good sniff convinced Sawyer a shower would be a kindness to his mate. Squeezing Dillon's shoulder on his way past, he didn't ask anything as silly as "Feeling better yet?" Not when the poor guy knelt on the floor in prayer to the porcelain god.

Sawyer emerged from the oversized shower stall where he'd been able to keep a watchful eye on Dillon. Everything that should have come out must have, because halfway through the shampoo he'd risen and tottered out of the bathroom.

Sawyer found him sitting in the kitchen with a cup of tea and half a dozen young men barefoot and in various stages of dress, sweat pants being the predominant garb on anyone who actually wore something. Dillon made a face at the dry toast Brad pushed across the counter. Trust the fox to feed whatever appetite Dillon might have.

"Feeling any better yet?" Working his thumbs into the big muscles of Dillon's back when he could appreciate the gesture had to be much better than when he draped his head over the plumbing.

"Yeah. No idea what brought that on." Dillon took another swig of the fragrant tea. "I don't think I've ever really been ill. Just woke up needing to barf."

"You didn't get stupid last night, did you?" Jerry spoke around a forkful of scrambled egg.

Dillon looked the other way before answering. "Nope, you and Troy drank all the beer and then played 'drunken hide and shift.' And don't forget to fix the ceiling fan in the bedroom. Ol' Horny-boy forgets where his antlers are when he's had a few."

"I only took one vane off," a tall, rangy young man with shaggy brunet hair protested. "And I'll put it back, promise. I'll go get the tools out of my truck, okay?"

Funny how the elk glanced at both of them while announcing he'd make things right but turned to Dillon to be sure how. Good, this group understood they answered to Dillon.

And Dillon answered to no one but Sawyer.

Life on the mountain was a metric crap-ton better than months ago when he'd had a mountain full of cranky shifters ready to tear each other to shreds. This young bunch were all Dillon's buddies, some from running the bar where Sawyer found them late last fall, and a few they'd acquired since. Wolf cousins Kevin and Jerry hung with the group more than certain factions of the pack liked, but the objectors could go lick their testicles. If Dillon wanted the wolves here, the wolves would be here. Not that Rudy had a problem with their fraternization. The Lobo spent a fair amount of time at the cabin. So did the Wapiti, leader of Troy's herd—and not solely because of the swing in the playroom.

Brian now—had he wanted to know where the up and coming power in the pack hung out as much as he wanted venison for breakfast? Sawyer slowed his hands traveling up and down Dillon's back.

"You're warmer than usual."

"Am I?" Dillon shrugged. "I just thought someone not currently in fur was playing with the thermostat."

Brad, now a slender man in his early twenties with a mop of red hair and a spattering of freckles across his turned-up nose, rested the back of his hand against Dillon's cheek. "I've heard of a fever. On TV. Maybe you have that?"

"I don't know. I don't feel bad now since my gut's settled down." He took another swig of the tea.

Good enough news for Sawyer to go back to rubbing the kinks out of Dillon's back.

"Besides, I don't know how we'd check."

A chuckle rumbled through Sawyer's chest. "We have a thermometer in the garage. I got it to test the optimum temperature for laying concrete."

Dillon jerked up, slopping his tea. Kevin, Jerry, and Troy laughed, stopped and then exploded harder than ever.

"Nope, nope, nope. We are not taking my temperature with an industrial thermometer!" The outrage aimed over Dillon's shoulder should have removed paint.

"Why not? You like big, long things up your butt." Kevin snickered.

"So do you!" Dillon snapped. "Let's start with you so we know what 'normal' is."

"Oh no." Kevin snatched a piece of toast out of the toaster and brandished the butter knife. "I'm a wolf. Normal wolf temperature is probably different than bear."

"First person who tries taking my temperature gets bitten," Sawyer warned. Maybe he shouldn't have started the teasing: this bunch didn't always remember to show respect.

"But it was your idea!" Jerry spouted with an innocence belying the flare of anticipation and power.

Just because the wolf knew Rudy was grooming him for power in the pack didn't mean he got to tweak the Urso of Ballantine Mountain. Sawyer captured Jerry in the crook of his arm, bending him into easy noogie range. He writhed under Sawyer's knuckles.

Sawyer ground against Jerry's skull, considering. With every noogie, he upped the ante. "First we find out what wolves average. Jerry, your ass first. Kevin, then you. Then, hmm, fox or elk?"

"Fox, definitely." Troy sidled backward, aiming for the door. "Brat likes things in his butt."

"You all like things in your butts. Show of hands, who didn't have something in his butt last night?" Releasing the well-noogied wolf, Sawyer glanced around the kitchen, noting the complete absence of raised hands.

"But we like big, warm things!"

"Or big, buzzy things!"

"Or bumpy long things!"

Now Sawyer was really sorry he started this. One Mazzola party and everyone offered TMI for breakfast conversation. He should have known. Weeks between full moons when he didn't have the bar bunch underfoot, and he forgot something so fundamental.

"Or cock! We like cock!" Jerry rubbed his scalp where Sawyer'd left his impression, mouthing off from out of grabbing range.

They'd run tonight in the forest. "We're going to have a house full of wolves starting around three o'clock, so if you want anything at all in your butts, get to it before you have more playmates than you want," Sawyer warned them. Not that Brad knew how many playmates equaled too many, but he already had more dick on hand than he had holes, so even the sweet, insatiable fox ought to be satisfied.

"We'll get right on that!" The way they thundered out of the kitchen, one might think there was more than one herbivore in the bunch.

"Get started without us." Dillon remained in his chair, the mug raised partway to his lips.

If he wasn't on board with the group jollies this time, Sawyer wouldn't urge him. "You know I won't play without you." He bent to rub his lips against Dillon's hair. "And if you don't feel well, there's no need to go join them."

Dillon set the mug down on the butcher-block table with a clink and swiveled in his chair to wrap muscular arms around Sawyer's waist. He pressed his cheek to Sawyer's belly, so huggable Sawyer almost wished for more arms to embrace him.

"I'm feeling a lot better than I was." Dillon rubbed his cheek against Sawyer's belly. "Just kind of tired. How much longer does hibernation last? I'd like to stay awake all day again. Maybe go more than one waking hour without stuffing my face." He took one arm back long enough to snag the other triangle of toast off the plate. He chewed, the motion of his jaw working the hairs on Sawyer's belly.

"Things should be easing now, pretty much done in a week or so." Sawyer comforted the young bear who'd just spent his first hibernation away from family. "Want to go play? Or more toast?"

"No. I..." He stopped mid thought, and snuggled harder. "Can we go back to bed? Just you and me?"

Like Sawyer would ever say no to such a tempting offer. "Of course." And he wouldn't even suggest sex if Dillon didn't start with the foreplay, or until the hibernation hornies struck again.

Though when had respites lasted more than half an hour?

CHAPTER FOUR

After three hours, should he start something? From the comfortable slab of pillow that was Sawyer's shoulder, Dillon still hadn't figured out what ailed him. He'd wakened ready to pounce on his big bad bear and wrassle the semen out of him and then... Violent hurling usually required a six pack of bad beer.

He'd eaten Liza's good food, washed his meal down with spring water, and hadn't had anything but some spunk for dessert. With Sawyer's full approval, he'd sucked off Jerry, while Sawyer pounded Brad into the couch, and then... he'd swallowed when he did Troy. Maybe the elk shifter had grazed on something nasty. Troy ate all sorts of weird stuff. Plants. All plants. Goodness knew Dillon didn't want a mouthful of foxgrass. Just a mouthful of fox now and then. Like when his buddies came up for full moon nights.

The noise from the other room sure sounded like they were having fun without the bears. But much as he loved his buddies, Dillon didn't want to be in the middle of the crowd. Or on the top, or the very bottom. Just... Alone with Sawyer.

Just the only two bears, well, bear shifters, on Ballantine Mountain. There were some of the permanently furry sort, but they probably knew better than to come near the house.

"...ran Brian and his little pack off this morning."

Oh. Yeah, that sounded important, and he'd been day-dreaming. "Um, weird. How many of them?"

"Seven." Sawyer ran tickly fingers up and down Dillon's back. "How's Jerry doing?"

Hadn't Rudy mentioned? The Lobo should be training Dillon's wolf buddies. "Pretty good. He's really hard to find when he doesn't want to be tracked, and you could say he's working on the badassery. I felt kind of bad for Brad when he demonstrated. We're all buds, but Brad nearly shit on the floor when Jerry flared the power, and then Kevin flared back for scaring Brad, even though he was half squatting too. I had to bust up the party before the fighting started. Jerry doesn't swing power around when it's just us."

The freight train grumbling through Sawyer's chest might be a chuckle. "And you? How did Jerry affect you?"

Dillon pondered. "I didn't cower, but... he's impressive."

Sawyer grunted. "It's different in a live fight. Harder to focus when someone's trying to rip your throat out. Hope he's got what it takes when the fur starts to fly."

Dillon hadn't even pondered the possibility of a real fight. "All the same, I'm glad Jerry's on our side." Like his best buddy would ever be anything else, not when they'd come through some crappy times and only surviving because the four of them depended on each other. Now he had Sawyer, and Kevin and Brad were paired up, even though he or any fox wasn't a prospect for monogamy, and Jerry went home with Troy. Heck, even Rudy'd gotten the stick out of his ass and Eric's dick in there instead.

But still, homes and lovers hadn't kept them out of a great big fuckpile: they were in it together. And they looked to Sawyer and... him. He had to be responsible. Sure would be simpler if wolves stuck to wolves and bears slept only with bears like the bad old days on the mountain, or so Sawyer said. Simpler, but not better.

And for the first time he could recall, he didn't want to go join the fun, even if the last tugs of winter were pumping up his dick. He had everything he needed right here.

He lifted his face to Sawyer's for a kiss, finding a stubbly chin to rasp his lips. Sawyer bent to him, greeting his searching mouth like he'd been waiting... And he had. Three hours awake and unsexed? They'd set a record for this winter.

"What are you in the mood for?"

Usually they took sex wherever they happened to go, oral, or hands, or anal, whoever wanted what just steered the other. Words to ask were weird. If Sawyer wanted Dillon in his ass, he'd grab the industrial-sized tub from the night stand and smear lube where it did the most good. Now he was being careful, like Dillon might break.

All because of a little puking. Okay, a lot of puking. Not like he'd heave again. Dillon felt pretty good, maybe not getting bounced off the carpet good, or swinging from the chandeliers good, but good enough to get down and dirty.

Except he didn't want fast and rough, or wild and crazy, or any of the things he usually wanted with this bear of a man far too tough to damage.

Dillon hated to admit feeling a bit breakable right now. Still horny though. "Um, I want to be on top."

Sawyer's eyebrow arched. "Okay. If you're up for it."

"I'm up." Dillon pushed seven inches of proof against Sawyer's knee. "And you're up too." He curled fingers around what would be way more than a handful in no time at all, semi-firm now and growing. "But that's not quite... Just kind of roll with me for a while, okay? We'll get to it in a bit."

Crawling up Sawyer's body made him feel like a cub again, finding shelter in a big tree, and nothing could get to him. Hadn't Sawyer gone out on a limb for him, making the elk back off? And the wolves? Pride kept Dillon from ever admitting how much he liked being protected, but... Sawyer was a den where he could retreat and be defended. He'd do the same for his bear, but... Was this what having a home and a mate was all about?

Not right at the moment, because when he lay on top of a wall of man like this, with their stiffening cocks next to one another and arms like tree trunks wrapped around each other.

Could he ever get enough of Sawyer? Sure, his friends had been fun when it was just the four of them, but none of them provided the same sense of rightness. Dillon brushed his lips up Sawyer's neck, trailing the tip of his tongue along skin. He tasted just right. Of warm man with the hint of ursine musk. Finding his lips would be a new kind of heaven, but even twice with toothpaste left Dillon unwilling to open his mouth. Sweetly tormenting an earlobe would have to do, and Sawyer didn't seem at all unhappy. Quick shivers danced across his lover's skin, and the hip action grew more and more interesting. Oh how Dillon loved being in the driver's seat with this hunk of man.

They might rub all the way off just like this, but Dillon wanted more. Something good, something they could both enjoy without him risking a gag reflex. Unsexy in the extreme, so what could he do with control, a handful of lube, and some imagination?

Dillon rolled them over and across the bed to where he could reach the lube and sat across Sawyer's iron thighs to open the jar. Damn but the guy had muscles on his muscles. His cock pointed straight up the treasure trail, dribbling a bead at the tip. A matching drip of precum fell from Dillon's own erection into Sawyer's pubes, not nearly enough for what he had in mind.

One handful of goo for each of them. His hands traveled up and down matching firm columns, pulling their foreskins up and over. Docking them meant moving, and Dillon wanted to be on top. He wasn't getting up just now, not when he could take both of their cocks in two hands—he needed both hands for the sheer amount of dick they packed. Rubbing on Sawyer had to be one of the six best things in the universe, and he couldn't name the others right now.

Sawyer gripped Dillon's thighs, the strength of his clenching saying an awful lot about where this fell on his personal scale of wonderful. Dillon bent down to trail the tip of his tongue up Sawyer's neck. Maybe the vampires were on to something—he wanted to take a nip and settled for sucking a rose of color into unmarked olive skin.

He could manage one handed while he fought the lube again—or could he? Dillon managed to get a sploosh onto his hand with the shortest possible lack of contact. Sawyer grinned when he saw where the slick went.

"You're hungry for cock today after all?" Sawyer's flip comment came with the little crinkles around his eyes that were part and parcel with the teasing.

"Always hungry for yours, big bear o'mine." Dillon lifted high enough—almost, leaning way forward to aim the monster—to position Sawyer's tip against the opening where he would push in. Dillon said he wanted to be on top, but nothing about topping. Swapping off would be for another time.

Oh, oh, the welcome stretch and filling. Dillon eased back, taking the long inches of Sawyer's dick inside, squirming and aiming and just about dying when Sawyer knocked against the best place. "Love this."

"Love you," came back in the deepest bass.

"Yeah." Dillon would grin except his face slackened with the pleasure and words went the way of the great auk, disappearing into the nothingness that was all sensation and love.

He could touch anything of Sawyer he wanted, and he wanted everything, long sweeps against chest and belly ridged with muscle, up over the firm pecs tipped with sensitive peaks. Sawyer hissed in a breath and tightened his grip on Dillon's thighs.

"You're going to make me come," Sawyer gasped, holding on for dear life to Dillon's legs.

Good, and exactly what he wanted, his mate's great pleasure while he took the many smaller bumps inside. "Do it, let it go," Dillon mumbled. "Fill me up, big bear."

Maybe he'd learn when to can the smartassery, because Sawyer could pound him hard from below, and he did, long strokes and huge crashes when hips smacked against ass. Fuck but he was full—Dillon wanted Sawyer to fill him completely. If being mated brought so much bliss, he'd happily lap up every drop.

Letting loose with a moan, Sawyer flooded Dillon's back passage with his seed. Pulsing and groaning, he stayed deep inside. Dillon sat back hard as he could, craving all he could take inside him. His own cock pointed half-mast at Sawyer's belly, but he'd engineered this for his partner. His mate. He'd take his own pleasure in a moment.

Collapsing, eyes shut, Sawyer whooshed a long sigh. "You're going to kill this old bear." He opened one eye. "But what a way to go."

"Thirty-four isn't old," Dillon argued. Would he be half the bear Sawyer was in twelve years' time? "So I guess you approved?"

"Agh." Sawyer shut his eye. "Do you have to guess?" He swallowed great gulps of air, his chest heaving.

"Nope." Dillon chuckled. Just watching Sawyer's O-face stiffened him some, but time to get off Sawyer's barely wilted cock—Dillon's favorite place.

"Give me a minute and I'll do you some good." Sawyer's hands had gone from clenching to caressing, wending up toward the business zone. He could linger on Dillon's balls a while...

But more lube. "You stay right there." Dillon parted Sawyer's thighs, smoothing wet glide on his bulging adductors. "Just let me get you goopy."

"Oh?" Sawyer raised an eyebrow.

"Oh yeah." Dillon lay down atop his mate, matching chest to chest with just enough offset to get his cock between Sawyer's thighs. "You're gonna hold me like so."

"So" was so fine—Sawyer pressed his legs together, trapping Dillon's stiffie between them. With long, slow strokes, Dillon pushed between those iron thighs, and he could have his way on the sensitive strap muscle on Sawyer's neck. Lifting just enough not to grind on his mate's spent erection, Dillon found a rhythm older than the trees. Held in arms even stronger than his own, he thrust until the spangles built behind his eyes, and cum shot out in thick streams. Sawyer held him through his exquisite shudders, and let him stay, face buried in neck, until he was drained.

With a puff of air, he deflated into a bear rug over his mate. Sawyer did the fingertip stroke up and down Dillon's back. "Definitely good for you too," came out with a chuckle. "Forget anything?"

His brain was a good grade of mush. "A towel?" Dillon guessed.

"Yup." Sawyer kissed the side of Dillon's head. "You get the wet spot."

⌇

Wet spot or no, Dillon managed another couple of naps, raids on the kitchen, and a blowjob fit to cross Sawyer's eyes. Whatever churned his stomach had clearly passed. A night in the forest under the full moon with his nearest and dearest netted him a haunch of moose. He dug up a ground squirrel he shared with Sawyer. Damn but being a bear was fine!

Not so fine the next morning—Brad went flying in a scrabble of paws and puffy fur when Dillon pelted to the toilet to give all of it back.

CHAPTER FIVE

"Hey, I am really sorry about flipping you out of the bed this morning." Round two of his morning yarking passed as mysteriously as it had come, and the dinner Liza set out for a pre-shift feast steadily disappeared into shifter bellies. Dillon ripped another bite off his third piece of chicken. He felt great now, if tired. He hadn't wanted to play with anyone but Sawyer again today, and long faces answered the news of afternoon delight proceeding without the bears. He leaned into his mate's solid bulk.

"I'm not mad." Brad dropped another biscuit onto Kevin's plate. "And I know you guys didn't really want company, so I got what I deserved."

"No, you didn't, Brad!" A year of living with the group hadn't cured Brat of some insecurities. Dillon pulled the fox into a one-armed hug. "I'm just a little confused why you crawled in with us. Or were shifted when you crawled in."

Kevin ran his fingers through Brad's curls. "I'll cuddle you any time, foxy baby. You could have stayed with me and Jerry and Troy."

"I know, but..." The lone fox shifter in the group flushed and busied himself dismembering another chicken wing.

"It's bothering you, so tell." Dillon didn't like "I know, buts."

"You'll laugh." Brad pulled the fine bones apart, not gnawing at the meat.

"We won't laugh." Dillon would personally punch any of the shifters who so much as snickered at the fox's distress.

Brad glanced up, his mobile face curiously still: any feeling would skim across his surface like a thrown stone in water. "It's just... I had a bad dream. And now I sound like a little diaper baby." He returned to studying the shreds of chicken.

"No, you don't." Jeez, if the poor guy didn't have the occasional bad dream after all the losses he'd been through... That they'd all been through, even Sawyer, whose lost family could be traced with the scar on his cheek. Dillon squeezed Brad more tightly for a moment. "Anything you want to talk about?"

Brad left off staring at his chicken, his green eyes bright and glittering. "I dreamed about my skulk, and my... my parents. My mom. And I was so... Well, I shifted because you guys take up most of the bed, but I wanted to be next to Dillon."

Really? Okay, if Dillon's fox friend found him comforting, he could snuggle.

"Because you smelled right. I mean, you smelled like a wet old bear, but... You smelled like..."

Like someone who'd run in the snowy woods in a heavy pelt and then taken off the fur and fucked like a rabbit. Someone who could use a shower. Dillon's nose twitched as he tried to find whatever elusive odor Brad sought in the night.

"You smelled like everything would be okay."

Jerry leaned over to take a good whiff. "If 'okay' means 'the mess in the taxidermy studio got cleaned up.' Whew!"

Dillon pushed his wolf friend away. "Not helping, furface." Especially when everyone at the table started sniffing for the mysterious odor.

Brad let his head drop against Dillon's shoulder. "You smelled like home."

Sawyer cornered Dillon in the bathroom at dusk. "Ready for a little pre-shift fun?" The waggle of his heavy brown brows left no doubt what sort of fun he meant.

Dillon thought for a moment. Saying "no" hovered on the tip of his tongue; he felt fine and not exactly horny. For the first time in months, the hibernation lust wasn't driving. He could say no, not feeling the usual, all-consuming lust. Or he could say yes, as his own idea, not hormones and winter. Well, mostly. Sawyer's smile did give him the best ideas.

Besides, he wanted all those kisses he'd turned away, plus some. He melted into Sawyer's embrace. Hairy chest to hairy chest, mouth to mouth. Sawyer moaned as their tongues met. Like he'd missed their closeness, more than anything else they'd done with their bodies.

When they finally broke apart, Sawyer mumbled, "Can't believe how much I want you."

Dillon let his hole relax, preparing for thick fingers and a thicker cock, but... "Want me how?" Dillon drew his finger down Sawyer's crack. His mate tensed and then eased up, letting him get deeper, nearly to target.

"Turnabout is fair play." Sawyer grinned. "You haven't exactly been lying back and letting me do all the work, but I think it's time you used that fine cock in me."

Good point—Dillon had been hogging the bottom, but... bottoming felt so right. The way he wanted.

And now his mate wanted something he'd be a jerk not to give. Even with anticipation tingling in his hole.

Back when Dillon still thought Sawyer human, he'd been so damned alpha. Who did what to whom depended on who wanted what and what felt good, not roles. The first time Dillon and his friends played with Sawyer, everybody'd done everybody every which way, leaving no doubt about Sawyer's love of a good pounding.

And every time for a week Dillon found himself ass up or legs spread.

"You bet." But Dillon didn't reach for the lube just yet—he needed more lips, more tongue, another long gaze into his mate's eyes before he dropped to his knees.

"You're probably tight." One slippery finger for Sawyer's butt, one wet mouth to slurp on his cock made for a chorus of moans above Dillon's head.

"Hell, yeah." Sawyer spread his feet wider, leaning with both hands against the heavy tile counter. "Been a while."

A trickle of guilt ran through Dillon. He'd been selfish. Time to make good with a second finger. Have to ease up on the tongue, though—fingering and sucking Sawyer at the same time could end things right there.

Dillon added a third finger, expanding his lover's ass. Leaving off sucking, he rested his cheek against Sawyer's hairy belly and wrapped his arm around Sawyer's hips. His insides made squeaks and rumbles to go with the deep throated moans coming from higher up.

Prep would be denial here in another couple of thrusts. Sawyer lifted Dillon to his feet like he was thistledown, a wordless version of "Enough already!" A deep kiss waited at the top. Phenomenal strength, used just to bring Dillon into mouth range. Dillon shivered, and shivered again when Sawyer turned and bent against the bathroom counter.

Dillon sheathed himself in his lover's body, possibly too slowly, since Sawyer shoved backward the last three inches. He'd not taken Sawyer like this in a while and needed to be gentle.

Sawyer rammed back harder. "Fuck me already."

If he flung himself back on Dillon's cock any harder, they'd both topple. "Hey, hey, easy now!" Leaning down to plaster himself against Sawyer's back, Dillon slowed them with one hand on Sawyer's leaking cock. Steadied, Sawyer let Dillon set the pace, absorbing each thrust. Dillon kept them slow until...

Oh Moon! Gripping Sawyer's hips, Dillon gave up thinking, concentrating on the slick slide of flesh in flesh, the pants, the groans, the "So good".

Deep inside tension grew. The feel, the scent, the mere knowledge of his lover. Joining so completely.

So fucking good! Dillon plunged in and held, every muscled seizing, and let loose, filling the most intimate depths of his partner.

Sawyer's cock jerked in his hand, throbbing, pumping out seed onto the countertop. Sex, and bear, and contentment filled the room.

Sawyer brought them upright to luxuriate in another slow round of lips and tongues that could have lasted until the sun rose again. But Mother Moon called.

Dillon chuffed a warning, the only one he'd offer before someone went sailing. The next wolf who stuck a snout all up in his business would meet the Claws of Doom.

Brad's loneliness had driven him into the bears' bed, but his insistence on Dillon's smelling right made everyone curious. Nobody got to put a cold nose there or anywhere else for the sake of curiosity.

If they wanted to investigate anything they should be helping Dillon look for mushrooms. Mushrooms. He wanted a mushroom. So. Bad. And he'd eaten all the easy pickings last night. The ones he hadn't snarfed up the night before.

Not a mushroom. He wanted all the mushrooms. Mushrooms!

Had to be somewhere around here. Rotten log, rotten log, where are de shrooms? *Sniff, sniff,* shrooms! Come into ma belly, shrooms!

Dillon ripped the log apart with six-inch claws. Tiny green plants poked through the crumbly bark, but where were the pale shelves of mushrooms? Oyster mushrooms came up this early, he'd eat them up yum, if he could just find them!

Not a single one on that log, and damn it, if Kevin nosed him again... Dillon took a swipe at his buddy. Dumb wolf got smart and pranced away.

How about this log? Or this log? Dillon left a trail of ruined trees to find the one miniature patch of mushrooms. He scarfed them up, and licked the wood long after any taste remained. More mushrooms!

What did Sawyer have? Dillon ambled to his mate's side. Wild garlic, early sorrel, nope, nope. Damn it! Maybe over here?

Oh, mm, yes, heavens, yes! The fungi disappeared, umbrella by umbrella. He wanted to gobble, he forced himself to nibble. Oh, mushrooms! Had anything ever tasted so good?

A solid wall of fur joined him. Sawyer probably liked mushrooms. He should share. But ummm..... These were his!

Oh, damn it! Big oaf just came in and took a bite! Dillon shouldered in ahead of him and tried to growl around the chewy, moist, slightly bitter mouthful. His! All his! But... Sawyer. Dillon quit snarling and backed away enough to let his mate take another taste.

But... but... he needed those mushrooms! Dillon snapped up a larger bite, leaving only fragments for Sawyer, and backed away, lest he trigger his mate into complaining about his manners. Sawyer was alpha, no matter what his opinion of Dillon's power. Besides, another mushroom clump grew over here!

The clock read 4:14 when Dillon wiped his wet legs clean in the mudroom back at the cabin. Longest stretch he'd been awake and outside since, oh, November? Maybe that was why his stomach growled. All those mushrooms were delicious, and so was the gopher, but such pitiful snacks for a hungry bear! Dillon skipped right past putting on pants and headed into the kitchen. Um.... Eggs, sour cream... Mushrooms! He found a bag of dried hen-of-the-woods a friend had left and set the dark morsels to rehydrating in hot water. Oh, yeah, time for a feast!

Sawyer and the gang turned up before the hen-of-the woods softened enough to put in the pan. Strolling in from the mudroom, Sawyer sniffed appreciatively. "That would go nicely with some bacon."

Dillon's stomach flipped right over at the word. "No. No bacon."

"What if I want some bacon?" Sawyer opened the fridge.

"Bacon! Yeah, bacon!" A wolf chorus and some hopeful green eyes demanded the fatty, smoky, luscious, horrible, nasty meat. What awful friends he had!

"No, I'm not cooking bacon." Dillon took the packet out of Sawyer's hands and shut the refrigerator with the toxic waste inside.

"Baaaaacon!" howled Jerry.

"Ew." Troy had swapped out hooves for feet and tiptoed up behind his main squeeze. "You're grossing out the vegetarian."

Jerry leaned back against his man, still insisting, "I am a predator, and I want bacon!"

"Enough!" Dillon wanted everyone out of his kitchen. Well, Sawyer's kitchen. Liza's, really, she ran the place, but she hadn't come in from playing in the moonlight. But he was cooking, he was hungry, and if anyone wanted anything they'd better shut up! Even the thought of bacon made him queasy, and the thought of the smell of bacon... He directed Alpha Glare Mach 3 around the room. Sawyer's eyebrows rose and the rest of the group went quiet.

"But—bacon?"

Damn it, just because Jerry was getting groomed for power in the pack didn't mean he could keep picking! "You want bacon?" Dillon yanked open the door, hard enough to drag the fridge half out of its slot in the cabinetry. "Here's your damned bacon!"

Three long steps to the glass door put him in launching range. Dillon heaved, and the packet of bacon sailed out into the night, far past the pool of light from the house. He glared around the room, daring anyone to say a word. "You want it, go get it."

Even Sawyer gawped open-mouthed at him, but at last— At Last!—everyone shut up about the damned bacon. He'd finished puking and nobody got to cook up a scent to make him start again.

"I'm making scrambled eggs with mushrooms and sour cream." He asked Sawyer in a more conversational tone, "Want some?" Just eggs, just for Sawyer. Not bacon, not toast, not anything else at all, and not for any mangy bunch of shifters who couldn't leave well enough alone.

"No, I'm good." Sawyer snagged an apple out of the fruit bowl and faded away.

"Um, I'll make some for us," Brad whispered.

"Fine." Dillon cracked eggs hard enough to split the shells completely in two and leave some chips in the whites. "And clean up after yourselves. Don't you dare leave a mess for Liza."

His mushrooms cooked up so nice with the sour cream and eggs, mmmm. He took his plate to the big plank table and ate in silence, while the stunned shifters sorted out their own wee-hours snack.

"What's got his panties in a bunch?" Jerry whispered.

"Dunno. Since he's not wearing any," Kevin whispered back through the click of plates.

"I heard that." Dillon shoveled the last forkful in. Mushrooms!

They stayed silent while he chucked his plate into the dishwasher and barely mumbled goodnights to his back.

Sawyer lay awake when Dillon slung his fully fed and very weary carcass into bed. And he wasn't at all pleased for the company.

"I cut you some slack in front of your friends because you've been sick, but I'm going to warn you once and once only." Sawyer could do Alpha Glare at Mach 8. "You do not take your temper out on me, ever. Got that?"

Dillon dropped his eyes. He'd really overstepped tonight. "Yes, Urso."

But Sawyer wasn't done ragging on him. "And if you want to be a good leader, you don't take it out on them either."

"I understand, Urso." He'd have to make amends in the daylight.

Sawyer reached out, though whether to cuff or cuddle wasn't clear until Dillon ended up against his mate's chest. "And since you're clearly feeling so much better, how about some blowjobs?"

When Dillon woke closer to noon than dawn, he very carefully lifted a puff of copper fur to slither out from underneath a snoozing Brad. With a fond glance at his sleeping bear and a gentle caress for his fox, Dillon started his morning routine with nary a lurch in his belly. Maybe he should put on some jeans before he headed to the kitchen.

Liza presided at the stove, with a much larger skillet than he'd used last night. Breakfast sounded mighty fine. Dillon sniffed. "Biscuits?" he asked, his hunger getting the better of his manners. He should have greeted the possum guest before following his appetite, but when the baking smelled so good... "Morning, Jack."

"Morning, Arth." The possum responded to his title with Dillon's own, meaning Bear in the old language of the Gaels. Dillon was Arth, second in command, to Sawyer's Urso, and better behave with more dignity than when he'd been in the kitchen last.

Liza peeked on her tray of biscuits. "Morning, Dillon. Any idea why there was a package of bacon outside in a snowbank?"

"Ah..." His resolve to hold his temper hadn't included any explanations for tantrums already thrown. "How very odd."

"It couldn't have been there long. It wasn't nibbled at all. I brought it in." She turned to show the offending package of meat.

"I see." And didn't want to see, because she'd snipped one end of the plastic open.

"I'll just fry it up for you fellas' breakfast."

Did bobcats toy with their prey? Dillon had never suspected their housekeeper of a cruel streak.

Which didn't keep her from peeling a brown and white strip out of the pack to lay in the skillet. The meat sizzled against the hot metal. She pulled out a second.

Dillon clapped both hands to his mouth and fled.

CHAPTER SIX

Once counted as bad luck, twice was coincidence, but three times? Dillon was making a habit out of this morning barfing, and it was time to find out why. Sawyer took a deep breath, told himself not to lose his lunch out of sympathy, and stuck his head into the bathroom.

"Did you wake up queasy, or was it something different this time?"

"Liza's cooking—" Dillon broke off to heave. "—bacon."

"Oh. Poor guy." But his reasoning didn't explain yesterday, or the day before, or, for that matter, why bacon had become a problem. Dillon loved the stuff. Sawyer pondered. "How many mushrooms have you been eating? Not all the varieties around here are good for you." He outwaited a fit of nausea for the answer.

"You ate them, same as me. I think they were all good ones." Dillon heaved almost before he stopped speaking.

Hmm. Sawyer forced his gorge down—if he did toss his cookies from the sound, Dillon's head was too deep in the bowl to avoid. "They haven't bothered me."

Hork! "Lucky you." Dillon flushed and sat back, tears streaking his cheeks. Sawyer wet a washcloth and handed the damp terrycloth over. "I don't think I can go back out there, not with the smell. Give everyone my apologies, okay? Liza's super brave boyfriend showed up for lunch."

"Gotcha." Sawyer offered Dillon a hand up, and to his surprise, Dillon accepted. Maybe he'd feel better after a shower. Sawyer started the water, and didn't debate when Dillon waved away the offer of back scrubbing.

He found the kitchen redolent with bacon and Liza building thick BLTs for everyone moving this early—all the house's current occupants but Dillon. They sat on barstools grouped around the granite kitchen island, watching Liza spread mayo and slice tomatoes. "Morning, Jack." He greeted his guest first. "Liza. Guys."

"Your Arth seems a bit under the weather," observed the possum. "Everything okay?"

Even if Dillon wasn't okay, Sawyer wouldn't discuss details. "Bad mushroom. He's fine." He poured coffee into his "Bear Hug" mug. Silly thing, but a gift from Dillon.

"But he's been barfing every morning!" wibbled Brad. "And he's so crabby!"

Why, of all the times Brad could have chosen, did he have to contest Sawyer's word now?

"Bad mushrooms would make you cranky too." Sawyer put a flare of "Shut up, Now, Brad!" into his words.

Maybe he'd been too directed in his power, because Kevin stuck his oar in even though Brad lapsed into wide-eyed silence. "But he's been doing it for days! Even though he's always hungry! And he's tired all the time. You're up and about, and he's been sleeping in still."

"I—" Sawyer used power and the Glare Direct on the mouthy wolf. Any weakness in his Arth did not need to be discussed in front of a guest. "—am a bear of power and experience, and of course I would end my hibernation earlier." And to put a stop to the discussion, he drank half a cup of hi-test brew. "Plus caffeine." He refilled his mug. "Dillon's fine."

Their guest laughed. "Well, then..."

"Well, what?" Sawyer's notion of guest-right could end rather abruptly if someone overstepped.

"Nothing." The possum jack lost his smirk. Grinding pepper on his sandwich absorbed his complete attention. "Nothing at all."

"Oh, it was something." Sawyer considered looming, which would backfire if he wanted information from this particular guest. "Do finish your thought."

"Well, he's vomiting, he's tired, he's cranky, he's hungry, and the bacon didn't set well, so..." He stared at the most well-peppered sandwich in the hemisphere.

"So?"

"It was just a joke!" The possum shifter set the pepper grinder down at last.

"So tell me. I want to laugh too." Sawyer wouldn't let the possum off on sharing his theory.

"It means he's..." The possum stiffened and fainted. He toppled right off the bar stool and onto the floor.

And Sawyer hadn't even loomed. Dang. That was the trouble with possums, stress 'em a little and otherwise sensible people fell right over. Brad flashed to the possum's side, patting his cheeks and begging him to wake up.

"Give him a minute, honey," Liza advised. "He'll come to without the fussing."

But the possum stayed down and quiet, long past the moment Sawyer expected recovery. If he thought playing dead on top of playing dead might get him out of telling his theory, he was much mistaken. Sawyer put his finger to his lips and got acknowledgement from his gang to stay quiet.

"*Zeep.*" Sawyer did a passable imitation of a cricket. "*Zeep, zeep.*"

Was that a twitch?

"*Zeep, zeep.*" Sawyer trilled again. If he laughed now, the game would be up. "*Zeep.*"

The possum opened one eye, casting about for the source of the sound. He noticed Sawyer and shut his eye again, fast.

"Zeep." Sawyer pronounced the word clearly. "You're busted."

The possum jack stood up, brushing at his clothes.

"Now, you were saying?" Sawyer inquired mildly, his coffee cup halfway to his mouth. He took a swig.

The possum hunched his shoulders. "He's pregnant."

WHAT! Sawyer spewed coffee over everyone and everything. "Okay. Good joke. Very funny." He grabbed a handful of paper towels to swab up the mess all down his T-shirt and Kevin's back.

"Glad you're laughing." The possum swayed a bit, oblivious to the brown drips on his face, probably noticing Sawyer wasn't laughing, not really. "Must be going now, thanks for breakfast, bye, all."

"Oh, no, don't leave us so soon." Sawyer left off his cleanup with a steely glare. "Tell us more about this joke."

"Ah, my wife, back before she had that little trouble on the highway, when she was pregnant, she had all these symptoms too," the possum babbled. "Morning sickness, cravings, certain smells made her queasy, tired all the time... Just a joke, like I said. Liza, you remember what it was like, right?" He beseeched the snickering bobcat with a wan smile.

"Yes, I do." Liza chuckled. "Love my kits, but wouldn't do that again for a million bucks. I prefer to be Grandma."

"Getting that baby born would really suck," Jerry observed. Sawyer flinched: he hadn't thought so far ahead.

"He can't possibly be pregnant, can he? Still, something's awfully wrong with him. Need a doctor, but we don't need doctors, much." Kevin picked up the thought. "Where would we even find a doctor that knew about shifters?"

"The passel in Possum Kingdom, Georgia, has a doctor. He's a shifter, he'd kn—" The possum cut off, two sentences after he'd taken the joke from funny to possible. "Well, like I said, Dillon's a fine young man, sorry I cracked a joke at his expense, terribly sorry, thanks for the sandwiches LizaImustbegoing kthanksbye!" He disappeared, and would have made a much better exit had he not dashed into the broom closet. After a series of thuds and crashes, he emerged, adjusting his dignity, and did a slow march toward the actual door.

Sawyer let him leave this time. Hard to do anything else with such a preposterous suggestion ringing between his ears.

In the deafening silence left in their guest's wake, Brad said, "Can I hold the baby?"

"Don't be stupid, there's not going to be a baby. He's a guy! It's something else!" The crew of shifters jabbered denials at each other while wolfing their food and scrambling to clean the kitchen over Liza's protests.

There wasn't enough coffee in the universe to clear the implications out of his head. Sawyer let Kevin take his cup.

"That's too bad." Brad swirled a dishrag over the counter. "I wanted to hold the baby."

Pregnancy being too absurd to contemplate didn't mean something wasn't really wrong with Dillon. Sawyer booted up his computer. Google-fu would find this shifter doctor. Too bad Possum Kingdom was so far from Colorado.

That's when money came in handy. If Rudy'd been minding the store properly, Sawyer'd have enough bucks to bring the whole damned passel to Colorado if that's what it took to get his mate medical attention.

That didn't come with seventy write-ups in the journals.

There'd be a hundred and seventy if there really was a baby.

Which there wasn't. Why even consider such a preposterous notion? Sawyer picked up the phone.

CHAPTER SEVEN

Not even noon yet, and Sawyer'd lost all tolerance for possum nonsense. First Liza's boyfriend, and now this doctor in Georgia.

Sternness brought no results: Sawyer turned to pleading. The Urso of Ballantine Mountain did not plead with anyone, damn it. And Sawyer still heard, "Doctor Livingston, I need you to fly in to Denver, and I'll have someone pick you up. Where shall I email your plane tickets?" turn into "Please, Doctor, just get here!"

And Dr. Dustin Livingston, annoying possum extraordinaire, pointed out three times, "I can't put an entire medical office into a black bag, Mr. Ballantine. Let alone make a house call in a state where I'm not licensed!"

"It's not that you can admit to this particular patient anyway, Jack," Sawyer shot back.

Calling him Jack changed the entire tenor of the conversation. "Urso, you and your bear are so far out of my catchment area, it isn't funny."

"If I knew of another doctor with your particular qualifications who was more geographically desirable, I'd be on the phone with him," Sawyer shot back. "I'd be happy for a referral."

45

A sigh from fifteen hundred miles away gusted into his ear. "It's not that I don't understand the problem, Urso. I do. And I don't have anyone closer to refer to you to, and won't unless I can actually make a diagnosis. I'll clear the schedule for you if you get here, and I don't know what else I can do."

And that was how Sawyer came to be making airline reservations, renting a car, and finding what passed for a hotel in Possum Kingdom, Georgia, Capital of Nowhere.

Of course Dillon bitched and moaned and argued the entire way to the airport. "I'm fine! I tell, you, I'm just fine!"

"Then you can be just fine in Georgia for a day or two." One more piece of lip, and Sawyer might lose his composure completely. "We're going, that is final, and if I'm just being a big old alarmist, after this I'll be a big old reassured alarmist." He drove all the way to the airport with white knuckles.

"I wish we were going for a good time," Dillon mumbled at last, somewhere between Atlanta and Possum Kingdom. "It's pretty around here."

"Maybe next time?" Sawyer smiled. Spring came earlier here, and acres of pink blooms lined both sides of country lanes. Oh, to be a bear in a peach orchard a few months from now! They'd have to take a weekend on the Western Slope come July—Colorado had its own peach orchards, and Sawyer wouldn't mind seeing how many juicy globes he could put away.

They found their hotel, a graceful old house converted to an inn, complete with a magnolia tree in the front. Dillon emerged from the rental car and promptly climbed the tree.

"Dillon!" Sawyer grabbed after Dillon's leg and missed. "Get down!"

The last thing they wanted to do in a shifter town where they were strangers was draw attention to themselves. They could both shield their shifter natures from prying eyes, but a six-foot-tall man in a tree eating flowers was bound to attract comment.

"But they're good!" Dillon stuffed another lavender bloom into his pie hole. "I didn't know I was hungry for these!"

"Damn it, Dillon!" Was Sawyer going to have to climb up and shake him out? "Get down here!"

In the end, Sawyer left him in the tree and went inside with their overnight bags.

And in the morning, Dillon returned the flowers, much the worse for wear.

"See, I am not being an alarmist." Sawyer handed Dillon a wastebasket and bundled him into the car.

2

Arguing with Sawyer hadn't gotten him anywhere: Dillon alternated between sulking and heaving all the way to the clinic in this miniature town. He'd been hijacked, damn it, and all he wanted to do was to settle his stomach and go back to bed. Instead he sat in the waiting room, anticipating his first ever doctor's appointment and hating every smell in the place.

He hunched over his wastebasket, telling his stomach to quit flipping around. The receptionist made some "bless your heart" sounds and waddled over with a wet paper towel.

"You poor thing," she muttered, nodding toward his trashcan. "I know just how you feel."

"You do?" Dillon croaked. No doubt she meant well, but this possum lady bulged about eight months' worth and he just had an upset tummy.

"Sure do, honey. These two kept me queasy for ages." She rubbed her belly. "I can sympathize."

"Thanks." Even the thought of two little ones inside turned Dillon's tummy another half twist.

"Saltines help," she offered.

"No offense, miss." He'd probably already offended with the "miss." "But I'm pretty sure I have a different problem."

She blushed. "Of course you do. I'm so silly! But they helped me..." She returned to her desk at the speed of a spavined penguin.

All the jokes Dillon endured the last few days made him jumpy about pregnant women. Gestating bellies everywhere! At the airports, in the town, here at the office... Here came another one! She waddled in, even larger around the waist than the receptionist. The, sniff, possum lady backed up to a chair, gripped the arms, and on a heavy sigh, sank down. If the receptionist had twins going, this lady had an army inside.

Best thing about being a man: swelling up with babies would never be his problem.

All too soon, or maybe not soon enough, a door opened and a nurse poked her head out. "Mr. Lawson?"

With a glance toward Sawyer, Dillon rose, and they followed the nurse through the portals of doom.

Stripped to his underwear and clutching his wastebasket, Dillon sat on the exam table fighting his stomach. The pictures on the walls weren't helping. Between diagrams of infected ears and cross sections of a woman in labor, he figured he'd be sicker after the office visit than before. Sawyer stood at his side, his large hand against Dillon's shoulder the only thing keeping him in place.

"It'll be okay."

A nurse in unicorn scrubs took his vital signs and medical history, blinking more at the persistent vomiting than at his bear nature. Finally she handed him a cup. "You know the drill."

"Actually, no, I don't." Dillon regarded the empty cup. "First office visit ever."

The nurse chuckled. "Pee sample. About half full, please."

"Seriously?"

"Seriously," came from behind him with a warning chuff.

How ridiculous, but Dillon dutifully filled the cup and didn't growl (much) when she stabbed him for blood samples.

Dr. Livingston turned out to be around Sawyer's age, a possum jack of gravitas and authority. And a definite whiff of a male partner, with whom he'd... Well, that must've been a great send off to the office.

Wait, how...? The doctor smelled of soap and cologne: how had Dillon detected traces of what the doctor had washed away? Dillon couldn't usually smell this acutely unless he was furry. Weird.

"So, you've been vomiting in the mornings, and are unusually lethargic, even accounting for hibernation?" The doctor ran down the list of symptoms.

"Yes, and eating weird things." Absolutely nothing could have kept him out of the magnolia tree. "I would blame the vomiting on the weird things, except first I woofed and then I chowed down. Um, magnolia blossoms aren't toxic, are they?" Dillon regarded the doctor's otoscope with some trepidation.

"No, they aren't, lucky you. Unlucky me, there went the low hanging fruit diagnosis." The doctor palpated here and there, and listened to his chest. Fortunately his belly had settled, though the doc must have gotten an organ recital.

"It's gotten to the point of people teasing me about being pregnant," Dillon recounted glumly. "Morning sickness and cravings. Even your receptionist was recommending saltines." He shuddered, recalling his companions in the waiting room. Two ladies, and who knew how many babies? Four? Six? More?

"Sometimes saltines help. Have you tried them?" Dr. Livingston laughed.

Sawyer didn't.

Dillon turned to his mate, now sitting in a chair to one side, and couldn't read his face. Except for the not laughing part.

"No." Dillon suffered to lie back and let the doctor press here and there on his belly, including the spot low down that made him groan under pressure. "Tender there."

"I see."

At least the stethoscope was only cold.

"You're sexually active, I take it?" the doctor inquired, listening here and there.

"Very. Um, it was hibernation season, hard not to be, and Sawyer and I are mates." Dillon decided to trust the doctor with some details, since he clearly batted for the same team. "Plus, we have some close friends..."

"I see." The doc took his stethoscope out of his ears. "I need the results from the urinalysis, and we may need to run a test or two. Give me a moment, please." He made a quick exit, leaving Dillon flat on the exam table. Would the doctor fuss at him for sitting up?

But, then again...

"Hmm, these things look like they're for feet. Bet if I scooted my ass down to the end of the table, we could have some fun..." Dillon wanted Sawyer to smile. Anything to make some normal here.

At least his suggestion earned him a grin. "Insatiable, aren't you?" Sawyer drew fingertip circles around Dillon's navel. "Save it for when we get back to the inn, okay?"

"Yeah." Dillon would. Because no matter how anxious this office visit made him, he still wanted in Sawyer's pants. And if he thought about what waited inside Sawyer's pants too much... Well, the return of the doctor would still deflate him.

Dustin Livingston excused himself from the exam room, because his professional composure started unravelling around the edges. Long practice at squelching grins and not dropping jaws served him well, and just long enough to reach the lab. Once there, he leaned against the counter and breathed long and hard, trying to wrap his mind around what he'd heard, with the stethoscope and without.

Dillon's urine sample sat next to the analyzer. Dustin could...

This flew in the face of physiology as he understood it.

So did shifting into a possum and eating crickets under a full moon—an indisputable fact of his life, no matter how much such things didn't get mentioned in medical school.

Dustin didn't have to ask Dillon to shift into his bear form to believe he could.

But this... Even with the faint sounds he'd heard...

Oh hell, he needed to know for sure. Dustin snatched a pink box off the shelf, tore open the inner package, and dropped the dipstick into the cup.

After a wait long enough for Dillon to sit up and snuggle against Sawyer's side, a rap at the door announced the doctor's return. Dr. Livingston trundled through, pushing a cart with electronic equipment.

"We're just going to have to take a better look," announced the doctor. "This doesn't hurt. I'm going to squeeze some gel on your skin and run the wand over your midsection here..."

Oh Mother Moon! Better look? Bears didn't get tumors, did they? Or did nematodes get big enough to see?

The gel felt like lube, but Dillon cracked no jokes about his belly being the wrong place. The screen on the device flickered to black and white life, showing blobs and globs in a triangle of light and dark. Hope the doctor could make more sense of what he saw than Dillon could, because he couldn't recognize a thing.

"What are you looking for?" Sawyer asked. "Do you have a theory?"

"Something out of the ordinary," replied the doctor. "Let's hunt a little lower..."

Oh no! Dillon survived his sleuth, met wonderful friends, found a wonderful mate, and now? "You found something horrible, didn't you? Am I gonna die?"

"No." The doctor stopped with the wand pressed about two inches below Dillon's belly button. "Ahh, a little lower..." He tweaked a dial and the picture clarified.

What pulsed inside of him? Surely not his prostate. Plus, his prostate only pulsed in the middle of an orgasm—the last thing on Dillon's mind. If his dick got any smaller it would be turning inside out and tunneling back into his body. What did "hmm" mean anyway?

"Take a look, y'all," Dr. Livingston instructed them, pointing at the screen. "I think we've found the cause of Dillon's symptoms."

"What are we looking at?" Sawyer asked for both of them. Dillon couldn't speak—his tongue stuck to the top of his suddenly dry mouth.

"Fetus. Congratulations. You've got a baby in there."

CHAPTER EIGHT

"That's not funny!" Dillon came up off the table at approximately thirty-five miles per hour. "The next person who cracks a pregnancy joke is gonna get eaten, I swear!"

Dr. Livingston and his Wand of Hilarity (Not) shot backward out of easy grabbing range. "I'm not teasing, Dillon. Urso. Really, I'm not!" The doctor pinned himself against the counter, shakily warding off both scowling bears with his ultrasound probe. "I wouldn't do anything so unprofessional."

"Explain." The bass of Sawyer's demand mixed with Dillon's slightly hysterical "How the hell?"

"I... I don't really know how," admitted the doctor. "It's definitely, ah, unconventional. But I've seen dozens and dozens of fetuses on ultrasound, and I know what I'm looking at here. Plus—" He reached out to something lying on the ultrasound cart with a trembling hand, taking one step closer to the bears and his possible doom.

"See?" The doctor picked up a slender piece of plastic. "I know it sounds peculiar, but when I was listening for bowel sounds, I picked up heartbeats. More than just yours, I mean. And doing a test seems like the simplest way to convince myself I was hearing things. But—" He held out the pregnancy test to Dillon. "Look for yourself."

"Give me that!" Dillon snatched the test away to stare at the pink lines in the window. Two of them, matching the printed code for fucking disaster. Oh, Moon, no! "This has to be wrong."

"These tests are 97 percent accurate in the first week," the doctor quavered. "And we just confirmed with ultrasound."

"This isn't possible!" Dillon flung the test in the general direction of the trash can. "You had to have tested someone else's sample! You have a pregnant receptionist! And another woman: they're about to populate the whole county with possums! Maybe theirs!"

"I wasn't ultrasounding someone else's belly," the doctor pointed out. "And that was definitely your cup. Had your name on it. You don't have to believe the test, but there's really no getting around the ultrasound."

"I don't believe you!" Dillon jumped off the exam table to loom over the doctor. "Everyone thinks 'Dillon's pregnant' is the best joke ever. And it's not!"

Suddenly he loomed over the doctor from several feet higher. Without even trying, Dillon put his humanity aside long enough to show his true self, his bear self. The doctor's eyes rolled back and he buckled, slumping to the floor. Where he'd be easier to eat. Dillon dropped to all fours, ready to take a bite.

"Whoa, Dillon. He's a possum, you can't scare possums and get them to talk sense." Sawyer smacked Dillon's shoulder, hard enough to register through his pelt. "Back off. Give him some air."

Give him some air, Dillon's fine furry ass. Give him some missing chunks to make him remember not to tease a bear. But his Urso demanded he give up his prey. Only for his Urso.

Dillon snorted long and wet, and backed up enough to let Sawyer bend over the damned possum.

"Wake up, Doc." Sawyer patted Dr. Livingston's cheeks hard enough to sound like a slap. "He's not going to eat you yet, so wake up. We need to get to the bottom of this." *Whap, whap.*

Dillon would do some whapping, all right, with scimitar claws. Damned doctor and his "you're pregnant!" crap! He reached back to get a good swing.

His mate put a stop to his attack with a sharp glance. Dillon dropped his paw to the floor, leaving five deep furrows in the industrial carpet.

"Put the fur away, Dillon," Sawyer grumbled. "Possums are hard enough to keep alert as it is."

Good idea, especially since Dillon noticed his skivvies had turned to a tourniquet around his hips even with ripped elastic. With another huge chuff, Dillon remembered where his humanity went, and dragged his human back on. He rose to his full height, and the wounded underwear fell right off his butt. He kicked the dead bikinis at the trash can, where they fell over the rim.

"Upsy daisy, Doc." Sawyer propped the doctor up to sitting. "Get it together and let's get back to business."

"Don't do that!" the doctor muttered, his hand to his cheek. "And quit going all bear at me! Jiminy Christmas!"

"Quit spouting bullshit like 'the bear is pregnant' and I will." Dillon still hadn't found the humor in the statement.

Dr. Livingston scuttled backward on hands and feet, away from Sawyer, still hunkered down for first aid. He ran out of floor and crawled up the wall to his feet. "Bless your heart, you think I'm having fun at your expense. I'm not."

Somehow or other Dillon got the feeling he'd just been called a raging idiot, however many benedictions had been wished upon his anatomy. "How else are we going to explain a pregnant male, except as a joke?"

"Now that I don't know." The doctor gave Sawyer a wide berth while collecting the ultrasound wand where it dangled on its curly cord. "If you can refrain from biting me, we can continue this exam and possibly find out?"

"All right, I won't bite. For now." Dillon wasn't so sure he wouldn't take a chunk out of the doctor anyway. "Sawyer, you don't seem all that surprised." He eyed his mate, who clutched both Dillon's hands like he wasn't too sure about not clawing as well as not biting.

"I'd heard a something once. A legend, like the White Bear of Bald Mountain. My great grandpa told my grandpa, who told my father, who told me. No one quite believed, no matter how many generations passed the story down." Sawyer gazed at something far away, or long ago. "About the First Bears."

"The First Bears were Urso and Arth," Dillon remembered aloud. "They were male."

"They were," Sawyer agreed. "But the First Bears brought forth the First Sleuth."

Dillon's memories of the bears' origins didn't include details on exactly how the First Urso and the First Arth accomplished such a feat. He'd always thought the stories were just stories, graven into legend. "You can't seriously think..."

"That we're like the First Bears?" Sawyer finished. "No idea. But we're the only bears on Ballantine Mountain. The only bears of our sleuth. And I know for a fact you've been puking every morning for days. Also, you're irritable as hell, and tired, and that Dr. Livingston's machine showed something he recognized. So shut up and let's figure this out." Sawyer's attention returned from the way-back-when: he stared holes into Dillon. "Not another word out of you without a direct question."

Damn Sawyer and his high-handed ways! Even with the old fireside folklore, Dillon being pregnant was still too ludicrous to contemplate. He beetled his brows and considered the likelihood of having picked up a nematode or something while foraging outside.

Even though he controlled himself to the utmost, Dr. Livingston approached with caution. Which didn't keep him from squirting more blue gel at Dillon's belly and smearing the wand through the mess while fiddling with his machine.

Once again the pulsing blob showed up. Interested in spite of himself, Dillon watched the screen. A little baby-blob? Inside him? For real? How?

"Head." The doctor pointed. "Heart, you see beating here. Limbs."

Sawyer's grip might crush his hands, if he wasn't squeezing back so hard. This was real. Inside him. How the fuck did this happen? Dillon clenched his teeth as hard as he clenched Sawyer's hands.

"Here's a foot." The doctor fiddled with the controls again. "Other foot. Hmm, little exhibitionist looks like a boy, see?"

Oh this was too much! "I can't be pregnant!"

Dr. Livingston peered over his glasses. "Generally I would agree with you, but we're looking at the evidence."

Sawyer squished Dillon's hand—he'd broken Sawyer's instruction. He wouldn't do so again.

"We are, but the question remains, how?" Sawyer stared at the screen, his lips parted

"Not to be flip, but when sperm hits the receptive cell, which here, I'm not quite sure what that is, and the results implant in a conducive location, which again, I'm not sure quite what we have serving as a uterus, but something intestine-ish. I'm not about to cut you open to investigate." The doctor scanned around for more details, none of which made any sense to Dillon. "I'm presuming you had plenty of sperm reaching the correct location?"

"Plenty." Oh damn, every time he'd presented his ass to Sawyer, he'd had a fresh chance... Plus their friends. They'd all played together. "Um, it wasn't all Sawyer's..."

"Hmm." The doctor peered over his glasses. "But Sawyer was the only bear?"

"Oh yes," they chorused together. Sawyer's grip became a caress, and he ran his fingers through Dillon's hair.

"As unlikely as a male pregnancy is, I'm going to have to declare the likelihood of a cross-species male pregnancy as so vanishingly small as to be impossible." He pushed his glasses back up his nose. "We have Papa Bear."

"Um, the opportunities went both ways." Was he in this predicament alone? Dillon dared to float a not-quite-a-question.

"Any symptoms? Queasiness, bloating, frequent need to urinate?" The doctor turned to the big bear at Dillon's side.

"No, no, and no." Sawyer did a double take. "Why would I?"

"That's what he said." The doctor nodded at Dillon. "It's now a reasonable question."

"No!" Sawyer recoiled. "I mean, no, but wow that Dillon's, ah, wow, um..." He wasn't saying "pregnant" because that meant speaking through the pain of Dillon crushing his knuckles into fine powder. Which didn't keep the smile off his face in the slightest. "I'm Papa Bear! Wow!"

"I think 'Wow' is now the acceptable medical term." Dr. Livingston clicked off his machine. "And we're all going to have a thousand questions, and right now, I don't have any good answers." He held up a hand, whoa stop! "I'm going to have to do some research, and probably still we'll have nothing but half-educated guesses."

Dillon wanted to ask ten million questions, all starting with how, and all stopped up in his throat. Sawyer asked for them both: "What do we do right now?"

"Go home and give me a chance to rummage in the PubMeds." Dr. Livingston unplugged his machine and coiled the cord. "I should have some preliminary information later today." He patted Dillon's shoulder. "Go get something to eat, try to relax, talk things over. Come back at three this afternoon, and we'll discuss things further." His smile was kind, but it was a kindness Dillon wished he didn't need. "One way or another, this will all be okay."

"One way or another,'" Dillon whispered. Somehow he didn't think Sawyer's idea of okay matched his.

The doctor crept close enough to pat Dillon's shoulder, tensed to run. "As a father, I have to tell you, there's no better thing in this world than going home to my husband and son."

Really? Dillon brightened. "You had a baby? I thought you'd not heard of this before."

"No, neither of us got pregnant, we had a surrogate."

A sharp bark of "No!" from Sawyer kept the doctor from being lunch.

CHAPTER NINE

So he'd been having morning sickness all along. Dillon clutched his wastebasket all the way back to the inn, queasy now from knowing he wasn't alone inside his skin. How the hell could this be?

Beside him, Sawyer drove, the wide smile all over his face mocking the whole situation. Big bastard wouldn't be so pleased if it was him. But no, there he was, all shits and grins and pleased as could be about this stinking mess.

Once inside, Sawyer scooped Dillon up to rock him like they were both happy with this fucked up situation. Dillon didn't hug back, and only after Sawyer forcibly danced him around their room for a good five minutes, to the tune of "We're having a cub! We're having a cub!" did he notice he was the only one rejoicing. "Dillon, aren't you glad we're having a cub?"

At eye level and close range, the truth sounded horrible. "We aren't having a cub."

"But... the doctor said..." Sawyer's brown eyes went huge.

"I know what the doctor said. But I'm a man, and men don't get pregnant. We're not equipped, remember?" Dillon pushed Sawyer back enough to not breathe his exhalations. Which were, yuck, bear breath, with this hormonally enhanced sense of smell he had going as a two-footer with a medical anomaly.

"But..." Sawyer lifted one eyebrow.

"Yeah, I know. But go back to the 'not equipped' business. However that..." Dillon didn't want to make the "can't be" more real by calling it a cub. "...got in, I haven't got the parts to grow it properly, and I sure as hell don't have the parts to get it out!"

"There's ways," Sawyer argued. "There has to be, or this wouldn't have happened!"

"Every way I can think of is worse than the next!" Dillon's stomach danced at the options running through his mind. "None of them good, and maybe not something I can survive!"

"Dillon, there'll be a way! I promise you we'll find a way. We have a doctor who knows what's going on." Sawyer tried to hug him close again. "He's probably really good at C-sections. If a more natural way doesn't present itself."

Right—being big and helpless and waiting for the knife. The nightmare got better and better. Sour fluid rose in his throat: Dillon whirled to the well-traveled wastebasket, landing on his knees. When he'd spat a last gob, he wiped his mouth with the back of his hand. "How can you think this is a good thing?"

Sawyer brought a glass of water and a towel. "A cub part you and part me sounds like the best thing ever, love." He knelt at Dillon's side and offered the water.

Put that way... Dillon didn't want to agree out loud. Drinking bought him a few seconds, and then he let Sawyer hoist him to his feet. He leaned against the warm wall of his mate. "I never thought about cubs because I figured I'd never be a father, Sawyer."

"We didn't know it was possible. Now we know it's possible." Sawyer rubbed his cheek against the side of Dillon's head, his words making little caresses.

"We know this much has happened. We don't know what else is possible. Or impossible. We're gay. We're men. Accidental pregnancies aren't supposed to happen to us. Families happen, with lots of planning and some outside help. But not 'Oops! Surprise! It's a cub!' And now we have the oops."

"We do. But it's the best oops ever. You and me, making a family. A sleuth." Sawyer's kiss burned on Dillon's neck. "Just like the First Bears."

"I thought we were a sleuth. You and me. Small, but a sleuth." Dillon swallowed hard. Wasn't he enough for Sawyer?

"We are." Sawyer pulled away now. Enough to take Dillon's face in both mighty paws. "Now we can be a bigger sleuth, with our cub."

"Sawyer, all I can think of is this—" Dillon stumbled over the word. "—pregnancy is going to kill me."

"You're my mate." Sawyer's voice dropped into subterranean growls. "I will let nothing bad happen to you."

Oh how Dillon wanted to believe him, but the something bad had already happened.

☙

Talking a pregnant and notional bear out of the trees wore a guy out. Sawyer was only too glad to tuck Dillon into the king-sized bed for a nap. Promising to forage for a cheese-filled lunch got him out of the inn for a few minutes of gloating alone. Cub! They were having a cub!

Dillon would come around. Of course he would. The shock was still so fresh, he couldn't see past the strangeness. But the First Bears managed! They'd brought forth the First Sleuth and retired to be constellations, bright stars in the sky. Urso and Arth watched over them when they roamed the mountains in their bear forms. How brightly they'd twinkled those few nights ago, knowing the blessing given to the bears of Ballantine Mountain. A cub!

Sawyer followed his nose into the A-OK Café, where some consultation with the young man (possum, actually) behind the counter resulted in pimento cheese turkey sandwiches and pita chips, of which a third disappeared before he got back to the Ashford House Inn.

He woke Dillon by wafting the sandwich near his nose. Hee! So cute, the sniff, sniff, sniff, open the eyes, sit up. No wonder Dillon had been such a grouchy bear: the guy was hungry! Sawyer figured the half of his sandwich Dillon scarfed in addition to his own made up for the missing pita chips.

"Better?" went from a query to a certainty when he kissed the streak of cheese away from the corner of Dillon's mouth.

"Some," Dillon admitted, scratching his bare chest.

Not good enough for Sawyer, who figured cuddling would improve his mood. Dillon had peeled down for his nap, and turned out commando after wrecking his underwear back at the office. Mmm, naked mate.

Naked, pregnant mate. Oh Moon!

Sawyer disappeared his clothes in about three heartbeats and slithered under the covers. "Come here."

Okay, Dillon might still be a little cranky, so start slow. Long, sweeping caresses, up and down his flank. Oh, his skin! So warm! And he smelled so good! Shampoo and man, musk and an elusive something that must be what Brad meant, about smelling like comfort. Like everything would be all right.

66

Maybe the smell of pregnancy. Of life. Of the promise for the future and of love for now. Sawyer never begrudged the frisky little fox any sack time, because that's what foxes did, but right now Sawyer appreciated the thousand miles between Brat and themselves.

Because now that he knew Dillon carried his cub, no one else could touch his mate. Not a wolf, not a fox, not an elk, not anyone. His mate! Carrying his cub! They'd damned well keep their damn paws to themselves where Dillon was concerned.

Whatever happened in the living room had to stay in the living room.

Sawyer wasn't sure he could keep his paws off Dillon ever again.

He pulled Dillon close, because anything less than skin to skin was unthinkable right now. Dillon rolled over, spooning into Sawyer's body, and tucked his hands under his cheek. Like he wasn't going anywhere or doing anything, but that was fine, Sawyer could get things rolling. Eventually. For right now, he needed to touch Dillon. Everywhere. Shoulders, chest. Belly.

A flat belly, well, except for the ab ridges, Dillon being a buff bear. Might be shaggy and draped with an oversized pelt when he was shifted, but as a two-footer, Dillon didn't have any excess, anywhere. Hot and hunky by anyone's standards.

How would he change as their cub grew? What would a little bear baby do to that flat belly and tight ass? The cub Sawyer'd put inside him...

"Moon, but you're sexy," Sawyer whispered, his hands finding slow paths up warm skin. "You're always sexy, but right now... You're sexier than ever. Can't keep my hands off you."

"Try."

Whoa. Never heard anything "no"-like from Dillon—ever. Not from their first encounter in The Bear Claw, the bar Dillon ran with his little pack of fellows. Not after what had amounted to a full-on orgy with the entire bunch, when everyone had done everyone, and certainly not after any play time they'd had since. With or without Dillon's buddies, who were shaping up to be Sawyer's allies among the other shifters. Hibernation and its unbridled lusts were over.

Sawyer stilled his hands. "The downside of spring."

"Oh, I am blooming, all right."

"I know." He couldn't get the gloat out of his voice. "With our cub." He squeezed Dillon a little harder and pressed a kiss to the back of his neck. "Our cub. That is the most amazing thing ever." Just the thought of making new life with this amazing, handsome, charming, powerful bear made his cock fill. Sawyer scooted back for enough room to let his rod expand. Dillon must have had the same notion: he scooted forward.

"You are the most amazing bear ever." Just as soon as his stiffy finished stiffening, Sawyer'd have his meat nestling right where they'd done their magic. "All knocked up. I knocked you up. Just amazing. Oh Moon, I love you so much."

Must be the big lunch sitting on his stomach, because usually when Dillon said, "I love you too," the words carried more conviction. Sawyer'd done the right thing by saving Dillon from those extra pita chips. Or he'd be so full he wouldn't be horny at all. "Just knowing you're carrying our cub makes me want you so bad." He scooted closer, nestling his stiffy between Dillon's cheeks. "I want to knock you up again. I wish every time I stuck my dick in you we made a cub. Damn. Just damn."

"Once was enough, thanks."

Yeah, once was enough, if it was the right once, and it was, hadn't they seen the evidence? And Dillon would grow large with their cub, and Sawyer'd have to lick every single inch of him. Because if he was sexy now, while their cub was little and blobular and his belly still flat, he'd be gorgeous with a soon-to-be-born cub rounding him out. He'd be miraculous gorgeousness and Sawyer would give him constant reminders of how incredible he was. Semen would make a great reminder.

Sawyer tried to honor the "keep hands to self" thing, kinda sorta. With one hand on Dillon's shoulder and the other elbow to lean on, he thought he managed okay, but he had to lean down enough to brush kisses across Dillon's ear, and the news hadn't reached Sawyer's hips. Just a little thrusting, nothing at all like what they'd do when the balls really got rolling. Lube would be good. Lots of lube, which was in the other room, so maybe some oral first, except.... Sawyer wanted to aim and enter right now. Did pregnancy come with a self-lubing butthole too? Have to ask Doc Livingston.

Or find out for himself. He pulled back enough to aim.

"Uh, wait a sec here." Dillon scooted forward. "Let's do it the other way this time." He rolled to his back and fixed Sawyer with a demanding eye.

"Um, okay." If Dillon really wanted. His dick was kind of floppy, so definitely some oral first, get him more in the mood. Sawyer wanted to fuck Dillon in the worst way, but this was the—the other father of his cub. "Be right back with supplies."

Sawyer unzipped his dopp kit, flinging toothbrush, deodorant, and comb every which way. Where was it? Then he attacked Dillon's toiletries. Nothing. Had to be here. "Hey,

Dillon! We did bring some condoms, didn't we?" He shook everything out of both toiletry bags.

"We haven't used condoms since we figured out we're both bears. Grab the lube and come back to bed," came floating in from the bedroom, with more outright pleasure than Dillon had shown for anything on this trip besides the sandwiches and magnolia blossoms.

"We need condoms!" Sawyer shoved his hand into a dopp kit, demanding the universe provide latex for his mate.

"Since when do we need condoms?" Dillon leaned in the doorframe of the bathroom, his arms casually crossed and one leg hipshot. "Lube's right there." He nodded at the bottle standing amid scattered toiletries. "Come on. I wanna bend you over the bed and pound your ass until your prostate calls my name."

Which sounded damned good to Sawyer, except— "Not without a condom. I didn't expect to have to get dressed until we went back to the office, but... It's a small town, shouldn't take me long." Especially if he skipped putting on underwear and socks, and maybe shoes too.

But Dillon blocked the doorway, showing no sign of budging. "We don't need condoms."

Sawyer pushed past him. "Yeah, we do." He shoved one leg into his jeans, and about fell over hopping to get his other foot into the denim.

"Come on, you're a bear. We don't get STDs, if we did we've already shared them, and a mess never bothered us any." Dillon turned to lean his back against the jamb, and his bright grin lit his face. "Getting dressed isn't how you get laid."

Sawyer fought his way into his button-down shirt, growling, "I'll be back."

"Really, no need to go at all. Come on, let me prep you." Dillon took matters in hand, stroking his cock to its full, impressive length. "You know you want this."

"I'm not getting laid at all without a condom." He did want what Dillon offered, and he summoned every bit of his self-control not to drop to his knees in front of his mate right that moment. But one thing would lead to another and he'd never get the rubbers.

"Why's that?" Dillon put on one hell of a show, sliding his fist up his shaft and over the purplish head. His foreskin bunched up, covering the tip, and then glory poked back through when he pulled back.

"You're not going to plow my ass unless you wrap that thing." Was this fucking blindingly obvious only to him?

"Never bothered you before. Why now?" Dillon persisted.

Slapping his pockets hard enough to sting his butt right through his wallet, Sawyer snarled, "Because now we know male bears can get pregnant!"

"But it's a miracle and it makes me so sexy and you love the idea of cubs, right?" Dillon jacked his erection. "You want to be sexy and irresistible to me too, right?" He took a step forward and his busy hand looked threatening. "We can have lots and lots of cubs together, right? Come on, we can feed each other saltines every morning and compare bulges and see who can't zip their regular jeans first. Peel down, Sawyer. It'll be great!"

When he'd exulted at his new mate's potential for alpha-hood, this was not what Sawyer had in mind. And still he took a step backward. "No, it won't. One of us at a time to be moody and irrational and swelled up."

"Moody, am I? Irrational? Swelled up? But that's so sexy!

You just wished you could swell me up with more cubs! Don't you want to be sexy too?" Dillon demanded. "So you're having the next cub and I can be all 'want you so bad, Sawyer'? It could even be twins!"

"Ah, ah, no." Sawyer tried looming to get past his mate, who was definitely tetched in the head from this pregnancy already. Rising to his full height and projecting enough alphahood to make every shifter between here and Ballantine Mountain cower and wet themselves wasn't doing a thing to back Dillon down, though he'd let go of his cock. "One cub. You're currently pregnant with it. We'll call it good."

"Now do you get why I'm not fricking overjoyed about this?"

Whoa, Dillon could loom like a boss. Wrath must've expanded him thirty percent. Fighting not to cower—the Urso of Ballantine Mountain cowered to no one, even, or especially, his Arth—Sawyer gritted, "I get it. Back in a bit. With condoms." He strode out the door, making Dillon move or get shoved, and latched the door behind him with a finality more crushing than a slam could be.

Damn, but he'd never been so glad to get a slab of oak between himself and another man.

Which didn't keep him from hearing "Don't bother. We won't need them."

CHAPTER TEN

Stupid, fucking, knuckle-dragging, shit for brains, self-centered, stupid... Dillon ran out of fresh insults for Sawyer long before he ran out of fury. How the hell had the dumb bear gotten him pregnant? How the hell could his body betray him by getting pregnant?

Men don't get pregnant! The number one rule of the universe! Not possible!

And yet... Dillon ran a hand over his stomach. As flat as ever, even after a winter of sex, food, and sleep, and more sex. And more sex. And food and sleep, which... Having Sawyer nearly to himself all winter certainly provided plenty of opportunities for this screwed up situation to occur.

Was there really a cub inside him? Its little heart thumping away in there?

Cubs were always for someone else, not him. Not the guy thrown out of his home sleuth by an Urso who thought Dillon polluted the hills for who he was and what he needed. Who he needed. Wanted. By an Urso who wouldn't train him and teach him what he needed to know to survive as a bear in a world that didn't understand bears. His parents hadn't been a lick of help, whether they wouldn't, or they couldn't, stand up to the bigoted waste of fur who'd turned him out into the cold.

A cub. For real? All the nausea was morning sickness? All the jokes were real?

Which—oh no. Heuking in the morning was one thing, expanding to the diameter of a Volkswagen was another, and birth—oh fuck.

Just growing this cub inside might kill him.

And Sawyer was so happy! Well, yeah, wasn't he the Big Studly Papa Bear? All "I knocked you up, I'm Da Bear with the magic dick-juice that puts babies in another man!"

Yeah, the second Dillon turned that idea on its head, the dickwad cried for condoms to save him from the same hideous fate. Big old jerk. He saw the problems clearly enough when his insides were threatened with gestation. Fucker.

So what could he do about this horrible joke the universe just played on him?

Things that grew inside where they shouldn't and threatened to kill the carrier were medical emergencies. Doctors were supposed to cure such conditions.

And yet... This... this... cub was already installed. And growing. Apparently happy. And Sawyer had put this possibility inside him.

With Dillon's hearty help.

Part Sawyer. Part Dillon. Entirely impossible.

But... A reality. A cub. Their cub.

Dillon's mama had sworn he'd be the death of her whenever his pranks got out of hand. Last he'd seen her, she cried while furtively stuffing his pack full of sandwiches. When harboring her gay son might have truly been the death of her at the paws of their crazed Urso, she hadn't given up on him. Mama Bear. Defending him, giving him time to run.

Dillon wouldn't give up their cub. His brave mama's

grandcub. Even if nothing made sense now. Too many unanswered questions. He glanced at the clock. Two thirty. Time to go get those answers.

Sawyer hadn't turned up again by the time Dillon dressed. Didn't matter. Dillon didn't need him and his attitude. Or his car. This town wasn't that big.

Big brave bear was sitting on a rocking chair on the veranda when Dillon stepped out in into the fresh air. "Ready to go?" Sawyer rose, keys in hand.

"I'll walk, thanks." Dillon marched straight down the path between the azaleas, jerked a magnolia bloom off the tree and munched on the tasty blossom while pondering the absence of sidewalks in a town where the residents tended to freeze up when a car went by. He got all the way to the medical office before catching another whiff of bear.

Dr. Livingston ushered them both into his office. "Shall we start with your questions or with what I've found? Because it isn't much. What I found on bear reproduction is quite different than human reproduction, and there's really no way to decipher how much of it applies to you."

There was no comfortable place in the office chair, or in his skin, or in his life. Dillon shifted anyway. "What I mostly want to know is if I can risk this..." he stumbled over "pregnancy", because how could that really apply to him? "Now that I know we might be able to have a cub... I want them." He wanted them with a rush of warmth nearly strong enough to knock him out of his seat. Sawyer crept his hand toward Dillon's, cupping his fingers where he gripped the arm of the consultation chair hard enough to creak the wood. "I just don't know how..."

If he didn't say "how to survive this" then his worst fears couldn't come true, could they?

And maybe the doctor misunderstood the nature of his worries, because he dashed on to practicalities. "We C-section about 20 percent of all deliveries, Dillon. I've reviewed the ultrasound, and I've been able to determine where the fetus is attached, so the surgery won't be complex."

"A couple of shifts and you'll be good as new," Sawyer put in. His eyes were huge, as if he hadn't really contemplated the things scaring Dillon most. Well, he hadn't, had he? All "We're having a cub!" when Dillon faced the hard work and risked damage no shift could fix. "I promised I wouldn't let anything bad happen."

"That's a big promise, Sawyer." Dillon didn't want to shoot his mate down completely. "Doc, how long do I have before this is a big horrible issue?"

Dr. Livingston rubbed his temples. "That's one of those bear or human things. Bears need about three months of actual gestation and have very small cubs, and humans need nine months and have much larger cubs. Erm, babies." The doctor shifted uncomfortably. "Is this something we could ask your family about? Mom? Sisters?"

"Oh hell no." A lump grew in Dillon's throat. "Contacting my family is a bigger problem than being pregnant."

"Bless your heart," Dr. Livingston sounded like he really was calling down benedictions this time. "We'll figure this out somehow. I've consulted with another shifter, not a bear, but she said to expect about a six and a half to seven pound cub. Um, baby."

"That's about what my sisters and sisters-in-law used to talk about. But I don't know how far along I am." How long had he been unwitting host to offspring in the making?

"Six and a half pounds?" Sawyer went dreamy. "That's big enough to cuddle without breaking."

"That's way too big to get through any orifice I have!" Dillon shouted.

"We're not talking a natural birth, Dillon. Your orifices are safe." Dr. Livingston patted the air, hush, hush. "Unless male bears do something we don't know about here. At least it's not twins."

Oh joy, a way to make the horror worse. Multiples ran in the bears: that's how Dillon accumulated sixteen nieces and nephews. Lots of cubs to dandle and snuggle and tickle and blow raspberries on tummies... And give back to mommies and daddies and run away home before diapers and bedtimes became a hands-on project. Though he'd been urped on more than once.

"I've never actually changed a diaper." Dillon followed the thought out loud. "My siblings are a lot older than I am, and I'm not much older than their kids." Four of his nieces were actually older than he, and used him as a superior sort of dolly when they'd played House and Tea Party. He hadn't minded— they'd fed him cookies.

"Why don't you and Sawyer come over for dinner? We can give you an inservice on our son." Dr. Livingston smiled indulgently. "He'll be a great hands-on experience."

Wasn't as if Dillon could go home and practice on the most recent sets of nieces and nephews. Plus, hunger would be rearing its head again soon, and damned if he wanted to be beholden to Mr. Unsympathetic for chow or car keys or anything else. "Thank you. We'd be delighted."

Sawyer could keep his double take to himself, and maybe Dillon could drag the conversation back to the necessary. "Back to how long I'm going to be...ah...swollen up?"

The doctor looked abashed. "We can't go by the last date of a period you've never had. Bears have this confounding factor of delayed implantation, so we can't even go by the date that's the likeliest, based on sexual activity."

"Every day's a likely day when we're hibernating," Sawyer informed the doctor, a big goofy grin back on his face, damn it! "If we're awake, we're probably eating, or ah, mating."

He'd been primed to say fucking; Dillon just knew it. And true enough, but crass when explaining to someone who fainted as a method of clutching his pearls. Well, maybe Mother Moon made Southern possums of sterner stuff. How'd he become a doctor, when every appointment ran the risk of him landing on the floor?

Dr. Livingston passed black and white printouts across the desk. He'd scribbled measurements for various body parts on the baby-shaped blob. "Your morning sickness argues for earlier, but the fetal measurements argue for later. If you were human, I'd estimate you're ten to eleven weeks along based on fetal size."

Dillon swallowed hard. Not blobs. His cub. His to protect, his to cherish. And Sawyer's: other papa leaned across the gap between their chairs to gaze on the pictures with his lips parted. But damn it, his mate better quit patting Dillon's thigh like he'd performed a clever trick by getting pregnant!

"But you're not, and frankly, I'm having to guess on what bear shifters should be based on averages of bear and human, and expected weight at birth. Is there really no one in your home sleuth who could provide better information? I could call them."

"No!" Dillon all but shrieked. Hadn't he convinced the doctor his family was a problem? One sister kept in touch, but she'd never keep her mouth shut with baby news. Or she'd turn against him like the others. "Don't call anyone there!" Oh fucking crabapples, his old Urso would send a hit squad if he even suspected the abomination he'd turned out untrained got pregnant. "If they thought for a moment you're calling about me…" No promise Sawyer'd made could be strong enough against the potential backlash, even with the entire pack of werewolves to help. Dillon knew how the pack was divided on the subject of bears, leadership, and probably whether or not the sun rose in the east.

"The nurse/midwife I found in Colorado is conversant with shifters. It's not like the AMA or other professional associations have a shifter specialty list. She's the only name that came up in a dozen phone calls who has OB experience with our kind."

"Ah, but she does have experience!" Sawyer pounced on the information. "Who is she, where is she, and what's her phone number?"

"Since I still don't have OB-type body parts," Dillon snarled, "what exact use is she going to be?"

Dr. Livingston went slightly glassy-eyed for a moment. "Prenatal care, for one. Margo Frost is quite competent to recognize healthy people, and she'll be able to identify most anything going wrong in the early stages and can flag me down, or her own supervising physician if you require immediate attention. You'll see her once a week, because we simply don't have enough data to call you anything but a high-risk pregnancy."

"High risk?" No shit, Sherlock. The "pregnancy" part, though… Dillon's insides flipped around. At least—the swirling, whirling maelstrom might be his own insides. Or maybe a future little acrobat in there. Moon but he hoped Sawyer was taking notes of the rest of the doctor's information, because

Dillon could only rest a hand on his belly and try to wrap his mind around being a father.

CHAPTER ELEVEN

A year ago only one bear lived on Ballantine Mountain, the last survivor of a once-great sleuth. Out of the blue another bear dropped into Sawyer's lap.

And next year there'd be another. He'd never counted on Dillon, and never imagined bringing a child into the world.

Who knew he could? He fought a smile. Somehow he'd hit the jackpot when he'd gone into Dillon's bar, determined to run a group of interlopers off his land.

Dillon snuffled beside him, stretched out as best he could in the first-class airline seat. Nothing too good for Sawyer's mate.

And Sawyer's son. His son. Soon he'd be a father. The father of his and Dillon's child.

He pulled out a pen and paper. So many plans to make.

Diapers. And childproofing—his city house and his mountain cabin had cables and outlets and stairs and... So many things to protect their cub from. He'd have no instincts about electricity. Sawyer would teach their cub about such things, and protect him from himself until he was old enough to learn.

Or maybe their cub was a daughter! Oh Moon, they'd have to teach her to be strong and clever and about being a woman. Sawyer had no idea how to start. Maybe Liza could coach? Good thing the girl issues were years away. Until then the differences were "pee up" or "pee sideways." Sawyer could raise a daughter, oh yes he could. Or a son. A cub was a cub—he'd love either. Or both. Did they still have time to make sure Dillon had twins?

No, and that was a good thing! One cub would stretch Sawyer's parenting skills. Once he learned to raise one, maybe he and Dillon could go for twins.

So much responsibility. Being Urso of Ballantine Mountain paled in comparison.

He'd draw up plans, remodel the cabin. A nursery. They'd need a nursery. And a nanny, one experienced with shifter infants.

He glanced again at Dillon, so peaceful in his sleep, and Sawyer's heart swelled. After years alone he'd found another bear, and not any old bear—his perfect mate.

So perfect they'd managed the impossible.

With Dillon, anything was possible.

After the peach blossom-covered rolling hills of Georgia, Colorado dressed in spring green looked a little ragged and dry. All the same, Dillon breathed a sigh of relief to be back. Dr. Livingston couldn't do a thing for him now, not when he'd finally gotten over the worst of his shock at a cub growing in his belly. Playing with a possum toddler gave him hope for managing.

Maybe he wasn't so adjusted to the reality—his mind kept slipping back to his friends and the bar and his responsibilities. And soon he'd have his hands really, really full.

"The Doc's son was cute," Sawyer'd mentioned when they strode past parents pushing strollers in the airport.

"He was," Dillon agreed, but he'd noticed Dusty Livingston and his partner Seth's little precious came equipped with a possum bio-mama who acted as a third set of hands. And who knew what they did during the day? Dillon tried to imagine any one of his friends as a manny while Dillon minded the bar.

His belly flipped like a pancake—Kevin or Brad or Jerry with an infant? Or worse—what had those fuckers done with his bar while Dillon slept and screwed his way through hibernation?

Their bar. Not his alone. But still—who did most of the work while two wolves and a fox humped their way through evenings filled with endless pitchers of beer and hamburgers served mostly as an excuse for more beer?

"You're not going to be sick again, are you?" Sawyer must have seen the doubts on one of his two hundred and seventy-seven sideways glances. He hit the blinker. "I'll pull over."

"No, that's okay." Midafternoon settled Dillon's stomach, even if worry stirred the pot again. "I was just thinking..."

"About whether Liza's venison stew will sit well?" Sawyer's knuckles whitened. "She said she put mushrooms in..."

As if Dillon needed another reason to regret his next words. "Thank her for me, will you?"

"Thank her yourself."

"Oh, right." If only because he'd left his Jeep at Sawyer's mountain lodge. Dillon could stay for chow, couldn't he?

Which brought up another problem, one they hadn't discussed to a fare thee well, unlike the whole "this could kill me" thing. "Sawyer, we can't tell anybody about this."

Sawyer did a double take. "Like it isn't going to be obvious soon?" He spared a glance from the twisting road into the mountains west of Denver.

"It isn't going to be obvious to anyone who isn't expecting to see such a thing." Dillon ran one hand over the six-pack soon to meld into a single two-liter bottle. "A guy goes bulgy in the middle, people assume it's beer." He pressed his hand flat, as if he could feel the small life somehow taken root inside. "And I don't want to answer twenty billion questions. You know people are curious, and then they tweet or post on social media." Dillon could only imagine Jerry or Kevin yelling across the bar at him: "Don't pick up that that keg, you're pregnant!"

"Whoa. Yeah." Sawyer's knuckles returned to the white and shiny condition fast becoming his new normal. "We've kept shifters out of the public eye this long, though."

"And we'd like to keep it that way." Dillon patted Sawyer's knee, the first time he'd reached out since getting the awful news. Sawyer relaxed a smidge and dropped one hand to cover Dillon's. "So we don't talk about this."

∼

Liza greeted them at the cabin in a wave of meaty, mushroomy vapors and hugs. Hugs? From their smartass bobcat housekeeper? Dillon hugged back, and frankly, he'd take support from anywhere right now. She'd been through pregnancy, she could probably help a lot, if... But no, they couldn't tell Liza.

Her hug came with an open-mouth inhalation, her lips pulled back. Dillon noticed her taste the air with a flehmen response before, hell, he'd done so himself, but only when shifted. Did the scent of peach blossoms survive the travel? Or was she assessing the state of his armpits after a long journey?

Liza pulled him down for a quick kiss on the cheek. "Congratulations. When are you due?"

Dillon nearly cracked a vertebra pulling up and away. "Do what? Why?" How could she know?

"Due. As in, have the baby. Silly bear." Liza smiled at him fondly, her hands like claws on his upper arms. "And do you know if it's a boy or a girl?"

Sawyer gaped almost as hard. "Whatever makes you say that?"

"You two silly bears! I can smell it. Once my Jack cracked that joke, it all made sense, I just had to believe my nose." Liza reached up to tug on Dillon's nose. "So, boy or girl?"

So much for not talking about his condition! "A boy. We think."

"Oh that's wonderful! I'll get started on baby afghans right away! How about variegated with blues and purples, two double crochet, chain two..." Liza fell into a yarny rapture, the very way Dillon's mother might have done.

"But Liza..." Dillon couldn't keep the note of pleading out of his voice. "Please don't say who it's for!"

She clucked and turned to the stove, where a stewpot of venison and mushrooms burbled. She spooned out two dishes of meat and gravy and waved the bears to the island to eat. "But you don't want people to know, I understand. Not that there's a stigma to an out of wedlock pregnancy like there used to be. Why, my mama would be cracking Sawyer's knuckles with a wooden spoon, telling him to make an honest bear out of you—" Her lecture on the rules of society came with a *thwack* on her boss's hand with her kitchen weapon.

85

Sawyer dropped his forkful of venison with a yelp. "You mean like you just did?"

"Why, yes." Liza smiled sweetly. "Just like that."

One complication at a time! "We're mated, Liza. Bonded, so we're good as married." Dillon would rather shovel venison stew into his mouth than keep talking about anything likely to give Sawyer more notions. "I mean, I'm still a man! And this isn't supposed to happen!"

"Darling, it did happen, so it must have been meant to happen." Liza ladled a particularly choice mushroom into Dillon's bowl. "And you are a man, a very handsome, manly man, or beary man, or manly bear. Doing the impossible, which has to be good for another hundred manly points." She poured Dillon a glass of milk, dropping a kiss on the top of his head while handing the drink over. She twirled away, singing softly. "I get to be the grandma! I get to be the grandma!"

Tapping at the sliding glass door interrupted her singing. At Sawyer's beckoning, Rudy strode through, dressed to impress in a suit and tie, briefcase swinging at his side. "Mmm, that smells delicious! Is there any for me?"

"You forget yourself," Sawyer snarled. "You wait to be offered."

Dillon would have snarled along with him, if not for a full mouth. Lobo of the wolves or not, Rudy presumed a lot.

Rudy stopped short. "Right, Urso."

And that right there explained why Rudy's control of his wolves sucked rocks. He neither offered nor demanded respect, and then wondered why wolves like Brian didn't give him his due. Dillon could clue him in, based on experience from tending bar. Start formal, then go to the casual. Start casual, the situations only deteriorated.

Rudy must've been a hell of a lot stronger than he looked, maintaining any kind of order in the pack with his piss-poor management skills. Honestly! Maybe he could teach Jerry the ways of the wolf, but Sawyer would have to be the one to deal with the wolfish-resources skills. Even if he was a bear.

Although Jerry didn't do too badly, for a guy who slacked off on the business side of the bar-owning as much as he did. Or had. A winter without Dillon to supervise might have taught him a lot. The Bear Claw was still standing, after all, and the books looked good on their last reconciliation. Damn, Dillon needed to get back down the mountain and see what havoc his buddies wreaked on their bar.

Sawyer paused, his fork near his mouth and one eyebrow raised.

Rudy snapped to. "Greetings, Urso. Greetings, Arth."

"Greetings, Lobo," came back in a chorus.

Would they skip the sniffing this time? Oh, man, someone already figured Dillon out once today. "Good to see you, Rudy." Dillon lifted his loaded fork in salute, effectively forestalling the potential disaster. "Have some lunch. Liza, do we have some stew for Rudy?"

"Coming right up." Liza reached for another bowl.

Dillon pretended he didn't see Sawyer's grumpiness, but when Rudy inhaled appreciatively, Sawyer's brows smoothed out. Guess he figured out the problem.

"Mm, delicious." Rudy tucked into the venison stew, bringing a hunk of meat and mushroom to his lips.

Damn it, Dillon wanted that mushroom! Only digging a larger cap out of the gravy kept him from snarling.

"So, who's going to be a grandmother?"

Oh Moon! How much had Rudy heard?

"I am." Liza smiled, but didn't offer explanations.

Rudy didn't ask for any, and offered a quick "Congratulations" between forkfuls. For once, Dillon could bless Rudy's obliviousness, because obviously, any grand-child of Liza's would be a bobcat and of no further inter-est. Idiot. No wonder Brian wanted to challenge him! They should probably consider themselves fortunate Rudy paid enough attention to know it was Brian itching for a change in pack leadership!

Once they'd tucked away the food in companionable si-lence, Rudy explained why he came up to the cabin in the mountains. He took a sheaf of papers from the briefcase and offered them to Sawyer. "The foundation's in on the bank, and we'll seat the vault tomorrow, the walls go up around..."

Any conversation starting with construction terms could last for hours and not involve Dillon in the slightest. Hibernation ended: time to get back to work. Everybody's work. Dillon had his own. He hadn't unpacked, and he didn't have a lot of other clothes up here. Heck, he hadn't worn a lot of other clothes while here. Most of his wardrobe re-mained back at the house in town, and might not have been touched since the snows started, unless Jerry or Kevin ran out of laundry.

Knowing those two, he'd have to retrieve every garment from the bedroom floors.

Dillon found his Jeep keys on the dresser of the room of-ficially deemed his since hibernation started. He'd slept here, what? Three times in four months? Home here meant the mas-ter bedroom, with the enormous bed and the even more enor-mous closets and the more-spa-than bathroom. With Sawyer.

Bears were solitary creatures. Mostly. Humans were a lot more social. Dillon had had his complete fill of sociability—just look how he'd wound up for consorting with another bear!

The Bear Claw needed him, and right now, he needed the Bear Claw: something he chose, something he built.

Something normal, like his old life, because his life would never be the same again.

Dillon slung a few stray possessions into a backpack and went in search of his suitcase. He strolled through the front door to drop his bags in the Jeep, and came back into the kitchen, where Sawyer and Rudy nursed cups of coffee while perusing the papers spread across the island.

Now came the hard part.

The big lug looked in his element: in control, planning, creating tasks for others to fulfill. How had Rudy not learned a thing from him?

Dillon sucked in a deep breath and exhaled slowly. "Sawyer, sorry to interrupt, but could I have a moment privately?"

"Yeah, sure." Sawyer made a note and dropped his pen.

Maybe he shouldn't have led Sawyer into the big bedroom, but superior construction rendered the room nearly soundproof. Dillon stood nose to nose with Sawyer, belly to belly, chest to chest, and brushed his lips across his mate's.

"Um, not that I wouldn't enjoy starting something, but I'm trying to take care of business." The swelling at Sawyer's groin felt like he might still be willing to take a little break.

"I know." Dillon kissed him again, sweetly and chastely. "I just didn't want to leave without saying goodbye."

"Go run your errands. Take the Escalade, it's still warm. Rudy and I will be done when you get back." Sawyer thrust his groin against Dillon's, giving clear indication of what kind of reunion he expected.

"I'm not talking errands, Sawyer." Dillon hated to say the next part, but he had to, now, with Sawyer still in his arms. "I'm going down into town. I'll be at the bar this evening, and I'll be living at home for a while. I had to say goodbye before I leave."

"Goodbye? Leave?" Sawyer turned to a column of cement—electric, angry cement. "Why?"

"I need to take care of business too." Dillon didn't back down. "My crew down at the bar have been carrying the load without me. My business is puny compared to yours, but it's still mine, and it still needs my attention."

"So, come back up after closing." Sawyer thawed again, poking a meaty finger down the back of Dillon's jeans into his crack.

Dillon shook his head. "I'll be staying at the house." The words came out wrong. "My house."

"Your house," Sawyer repeated, his eyebrows inching toward his hairline.

"Yes, my house, where I live with my friends and co-owners." Had Sawyer really forgotten about Dillon's life before hibernation?

"Why?" Close quarters turned a shout into a roar.

Dillon refused to flinch. He did step back, the better to draw to full height and state his case. And get Sawyer's hand out of the distraction zone. "Because I need to take care of my business the same way you need to take care of yours. And—because I need some space here, Sawyer."

"But..." Sawyer faltered. "Our cub..."

"Is perfectly safe where he is," Dillon reminded him. At least, as perfectly safe as he could be in a body not meant for the task.

"But you're taking him away!" came out on a low growl.

"I'd be perfectly happy to teleport him into your belly," Dillon reminded Sawyer, and tried to stamp down the flame of satisfaction at his flinch. "I need a couple of days where nobody's staring at me or getting giddy about cubs or trying to figure out how I got into this ridiculous situation. I need something of my own life back, for the little while I can have it, because my life is never going to be the same again."

"What if your Urso demands you stay?" Sawyer rumbled.

"I thought you were better than my old Urso," Dillon shot back. "And if you're not, you're due for a challenge. What's the protocol? Claws at dawn?"

He may as well have stuck a claw into a balloon, the way Sawyer deflated. "I'm sorry. That was unworthy of me. But I don't want you to go."

He stepped against Sawyer again and tried to reassure him with a kiss. "It's just for a while. But I need some time." He didn't want to say "away from you," though no denying the truth. "You'll be coming through on your way back to the city. Stop in. We'll figure something out."

"I don't like separating our family." Sawyer wrapped his arms around Dillon, crushing him against his burly torso. "I love you."

Staying or going wasn't a question of love, and never had been. "I love you too, Sawyer." Dillon clung tightly, suddenly aware how he'd be giving up the solid wall of defense against the world in the form of his big, strong bear lover. "And our cub is as safe with me as he possibly can be."

Damn, he'd chosen a time to go when Rudy and the paperwork would keep Sawyer from dropping their britches and making a leisurely goodbye—a stupid mistake. Except intimacy would be the perfect way to undermine his resolve. Dillon broke their embrace, leaving Sawyer with the only comfort he could find. "I'll see you soon. Start thinking up real names for Boo-Boo, okay?"

The silly name brought traces of a smile. But only the traces. Dillon left before he could change his mind and stay.

2

Sawyer clenched his fists until they ached. How could Dillon simply walk out, for a day or a week, or...? He said it wasn't forever, he said just for a bit. For time to think. But— How could he go?

Even for a day or a week? Didn't he know how badly he'd jerked Sawyer's heart right out of his chest?

But he'd named their cub. With a silly, affectionate, "we don't know who you are yet" name.

Sawyer wanted to roar, he wanted to shift, he wanted to tear apart trees and overturn boulders with his six-inch scimitars. He wanted to make Nature pay for playing a joke on Dillon, making him go away. He wanted—

He wanted Dillon. And he wanted to be a better Urso than the only other bear leader Dillon had ever known.

Sawyer had to let Dillon leave.

But he didn't have to like it!

Sawyer stalked back into the kitchen while Rudy was finishing off the last of an entire pot of coffee. No coffee, no Dillon, no patience, no... Sawyer examined the empty carafe and threw the useless, empty thing into the sink harder than the glass could take. Shards flew and landed with a tinkle.

Fuck it. Sawyer tromped back to the island and crashed into his seat. He snatched an estimate out of Rudy's hand, grabbing hard enough to make that jackass of a wolf slop the last of the coffee over the edge of his cup.

"Something wrong?" Rudy didn't back down from an angry bear, being either a fool or an alpha.

"No!" Sawyer wasn't about to tell the miserable cur Dillon wasn't coming back to the cabin any time soon, and he'd promised not to talk about the reason why. "Not a Moon-cursed thing is wrong!"

Dillon reached the Bear Claw early enough to catch only the owners there, cutting limes and stocking the cooler. "Hi, guys! You put anything new on the menu?"

"Hah hah!" Kevin, Jerry, and Brad ran to hug Dillon in the sort of puppypile he'd depended on for affection until a bear walked into their bar last winter. Dillon wouldn't think of Sawyer now, not when his best buddies in all the world hugged on him and thumped on him, so, so glad to see him.

"Jerry only burns one burger out of four these days!" Brad wormed his way through the group embrace to end under Dillon's arm.

"Got a new flavor of barbecue sauce to hide the char, too!" Jerry didn't deny his beef-scorching ways and managed to hug both Dillon and Brad. "A complimentary shooter for whoever gets the burnt one keeps the complaints down."

His arms full of his friends, Dillon laughed and squeezed. Home. Both the bar and Sawyer's cabin were home. He was back in his old life, with new life, and a hole in his heart he could plaster over with—

With nothing and no one. Only Sawyer fit there, and Sawyer went and knocked him up. Dillon needed more time to come to terms with the fantastic upending of life as he knew it, but he wasn't lying, he needed not to look at Sawyer, all giddy and apologetic and giddy again, while he worked things out in his head.

He'd hemmed himself in by making Sawyer promise not to tell anyone about their cub—he couldn't tell his friends either. Maybe he could talk to the nurse practitioner when he went in for his appointments, though a stranger wouldn't be the same.

Right now he had his buddies and the joy of being back on his own turf. The gouges in the doorframe where he'd clawed the wood were just as deep, the scratches in the bar a little deeper, and the burned-out light on the jukebox still needed replacing on B-17. Some things never changed, even when everything else did.

Brad snuffled hard—so glad to see Dillon he cried? They'd seen each other a few days ago! But no—Brad pulled his lips back in a flehmen, just the way Liza had. Kevin and Jerry took deep whiffs too.

"Are you okay?" Brad peered up through a mop of ginger curls to meet Dillon's eyes.

"I'm fine, Brat." Dillon dropped a kiss into the copper mass. He was, he really was, and he wouldn't start expanding for a while—which would bring the awkward questions he could delay for now. "I got an explanation for the barfing. No big, even if it happens some more."

"Good." Brad snuggled tighter, sniffing more deeply. "You will let me hold the baby, won't you?"

Oh man. They knew. Relief shook Dillon's shoulders, with every doubt about his crazy pregnancy, until he turned into a quaking mass whose knees weren't holding too well. Dillon leaned more on Brad than the little fox could take, but Kevin and Jerry propped him up. They knew. And they still held him, even through the murmur of questions. Every doubt quaked him until they spouted out his eyes and stole most of his voice. He wept, for the crazy fucked up situation and for missing Sawyer and for Sawyer doing this to him, and for friends who'd hold him while he wept.

"Sure, Brad," Dillon finally choked out. "You can hold the baby."

CHAPTER TWELVE

Sawyer strolled through the house he'd once been so proud of. If his heart grew any heavier he'd haul the damned thing around in his jeans.

Liza spent the afternoon with her Jack, leaving the kitchen empty and quiet. No Jerry, Kevin, Brad, Troy, Eric, or even Rudy. And worst of all, no Dillon.

He stepped into his beautifully arranged office. A random stack of papers on one corner of his desk wouldn't stay there three minutes' past Dillon seeing it. The management textbooks his bear purchased for his online studies could be relegated to a low bookshelf—surely Dillon wouldn't have time for such once their cub was born.

The Bear Claw might need a new name as well; Dillon wouldn't remain with the bar once he had parental responsibilities, would he? Their cub would need him home in the evenings. So would Sawyer.

Sawyer could manage all their financial needs—he made a damned good provider, with the means to keep his family comfortable.

Of course, Sawyer might have to make a few changes in his own life. Starting with the playroom. Oh, dear Moon! A swing! Riding crops! An entire porn shop of sex toys and lube ordered by the case, by wolves and foxes and pumas who had some strange ideas about what Sawyer actually liked.

Well, it had come in quite handy for political matters, but Rudy and Eric were settled now, and they could play on their own turf. Boo-Boo would just treat the whipping rack like an indoor tree, and climb.

Not suitable at all for their cub! Rudy and Eric could take these toys away to their own home: a toy chest in here should contain plushies and Legos and puzzles! He'd be a father soon, and he and Dillon would raise their son here, together.

Well, the space served as a grownup playroom long enough. He returned to his office for pencil and paper. Where to begin? A few favorite items under lock and key in his and Dillon's bedroom. The rest?

Whatever Rudy and Eric didn't take could be a gift to the foxes.

Once he cleared out the space, he'd cut an opening on the far wall, put in a door for easy access to his and Dillon's bedroom.

He'd add a wall...here...dividing the space into a nursery and a playroom. Hmmm... For too long his workshop out back sat idle. An image appeared in his mind, a copy of something he'd seen long ago at his grandparents' house.

"Liza was here" might as well have hung on a sign over the door, for his neglected tools sported no dust, and the walnut slabs he'd saved for a special occasion sat stacked by the door. Tongue stuck out from between his teeth, he sketched out the crib he'd build.

Then a changing table. A dresser.

Oh! A rocking bear! Like the one he'd loved when a cub himself.

Come Monday he'd need to rejoin the world, play human businessman again. But his weekend? He could either sit around drinking and moping over his absent lover, or...

He could make the next Ballantine a room to be proud of.

Liza's handmade afghan would look so good against the walnut.

Wouldn't Dillon be surprised?

If, no, when, he came home.

The last nip of winter swirled in the wind, blown down from the mountains to the western edge of the city. The fresh green scents of pine and sage were lost in the asphalt, exhaust, and machine oil of the construction site. Sawyer considered buttoning up his jacket, more for the benefit of the human types currently installing electrical cable in the structure than for his own comfort. The exterior walls still lacked windows, and flooring would go over the visible tangle of ductwork and wires.

His building had grown over the winter under Rudy's supervision. Sawyer'd spent most of his time rolling in the sack with the cranky-ass bear not currently living with him, but Sawyer'd also spent a certain amount of awake time looking at blueprints and specs and cutting some checks for materials intended to become a bank. He'd looked after business, best he could while in the throes of hibernation.

And now, when he could spend his full daytime energies on making his construction company a success, no one waited at home for him to bring the details to. Dillon took days to answer any texts, wouldn't pick up the phone when

Sawyer called, and when he returned a call at his own good pace, Sawyer fought the urge to tear a strip of fur and hide off him.

The one time he'd tried, Dillon had gone all "Yes, Urso, no, Urso, anything you say, Urso." Like Sawyer was the exact replica of the bad leader who'd cast Dillon out of his home sleuth.

Which made Sawyer all the madder for Dillon's being right. As Arth, he remained loyal and obedient. As mate and parent to their cub, he wouldn't stand for nonsense. Damn it! Who knew being a family took so much patience?

Being a boss presented some of the same challenges, but with a lot more scope for issuing orders and making demands. And Sawyer demanded a lot from his crews and contractors, which built his company into the thriving operation currently building a branch office for a national banking chain.

And why Sawyer halted the threading of electrical wire through conduit. The electrician stopped his work at Sawyer's question. "What kind of wire is this?"

"Milex 3. A little light for this application, if you ask me, but it's what TJ said to use." The electrician took a pull from a water bottle.

"How much is already laid down?" Sawyer gritted his teeth, wishing he had the other electrician between his jaws. A little light for the application? Try not even close to what he'd spec'ed and paid for! He seized the cable to shake and glare, as if his righteous anger might magically turn tinsel into the DK 4 he'd bought.

"Part of the first floor." The electrician shrugged. "It'll do the job, if they don't overload it."

"Damn it!" Since a robbery would overload the conduit, with the vaults needing to swing their thousand pound doors shut, the building would fail catastrophically. Sawyer left off punishing the cable to hunt for the foreman. He bellowed, "Rudy!"

The Lobo of the wolves and site supervisor stuck his head out from behind the vault, the centerpiece of the entire structure. "What?"

"What the hell is with the Milex?" Itching to shift and pummel his subordinate for screwing with the site, Sawyer chuffed hard enough to lift Rudy's hair.

"What Milex?" he asked, bristling back. "We took delivery of four spools of DK 4."

"Oh hell no." Sawyer grabbed Rudy's arm and dragged him willy-nilly to the back dock where the cable waited. "What color is DK 4?"

"I dunno." Rudy jerked his arm back, or tried to. Sawyer considered shifting one limb and taking a slash at his foreman for being stupid. He settled for gripping harder. "The spools said DK 4, we signed for DK 4. What's your problem?"

"The problem—" Sawyer all but flung the wolf at the first huge spool. "—is that DK 4 is green. This, if you will look closely, is chartreuse, and the copper inside is thinner. The electrician noticed, I noticed, and you can be damned well sure whoever has the DK 4 I paid a frickin' fortune for noticed too!"

"Back off, Sawyer." Rudy flared power, enough to remind the bear he was roughing up an alpha. "Look at the spools. DK 4."

"Look at the cable!" Sawyer demanded, shoving the end into Rudy's mitt.

"Fuck." Rudy quit posturing enough to examine the cut end. "This isn't..."

"Damn right it isn't." Sawyer's height allowed him to see the label on the top of the spool without lifting to his toes. "But the label sure says it is."

Mother Moon curse it, the difference between four spools of the two products equaled thousands of dollars. More than enough to make pulling a switch worth some unscrupulous shit's time.

"Where did this come from?" Sawyer rounded on Rudy, still staring stupidly at the chartreuse cable with twists of copper poking out the end. "The substitution wasn't done on site. The spools are too massive to handle without the truck and forklift, even for me. It wasn't done at the manufacturer—they aren't made by the same company. So it has to have been mislabeled at the supplier and sent out from there. And there's no way this was an accident."

"No! I checked off the DK 4 when it came in!" Rudy dropped the end of the cable. He tensed and sprang, wolf-like, to the top of the spool. He knelt atop the plywood, staring at the laminated placard proclaiming the wire type. No mere human could have made the standing leap to a platform at Sawyer's nose-level. Rudy was no human, but Sawyer's estimation of him as an alpha and as a supervisor dropped faster than clothes at shifting time.

"Look, I initialed the type..." Rudy's voice trailed off. He scrabbled at the edge of the placard. It lifted away from the spool, yielding the truth. Another card, smaller, stapled to the plywood, told the cable's true origin. "Damn it!"

Sawyer snatched the placard out of Rudy's hand, not even waiting for the Lobo to jump back to the ground. "Fuck! Where did we get this? WLFS Supply, right?"

"Yeah," Rudy grunted, landing a little harder than he might have a year ago. "You like to keep work in the family, remember?"

"We're about to have a major redefinition of family in about fifteen minutes." Sawyer sliced off a foot of cable, snapped half a dozen pictures of the spools, with his cell phone and turned on his heel. He strode through the work site, his skin tingling with the need to let his fur out and his claws lengthen. The better to smash the electrician away from his work before one more foot of cable got laid. "Take the rest of the day off," he growled on his way past, batting the man away with words alone. "We may have to pull everything on the first floor."

"Okay, boss." The startled electrician dropped the char-treuse cable. "Hey, Rudy, do I still get paid?"

Sawyer hadn't bothered to check if his foreman followed, though he'd better not do anything else. One thing right—Rudy answered from behind him. Wrong answer, though—"No."

"Yes, he does!" Sawyer snarled, never looking back.

"Okay!" Rudy's footsteps had sped up, like he might try to match Sawyer stride for stride to the Escalade, and then slowed again, keeping his distance.

But still following. Good. Shithead had to remember who ran this company, who ran the mountain, who kept his sorry ass employed and head of the pack. Rudy barely parked his butt in the seat when Sawyer peeled the massive SUV out of the worksite and down the highway.

"That electrician doesn't pay for your mistake. You do." Sawyer finally spoke, halfway to the warehouse. He sped around an eighteen-wheeler and a much smaller SUV, enjoying the way Rudy dug his fingers into the black leather of the seat and the whiff of fear. "I do not pay for your mistake. I pay you to keep mistakes from happening. Which you have not. Fix. It."

Slamming into a front-door parking space and jerking out of gear hard enough to fling Rudy back and forth, Sawyer braced to tear WLFS Supply to the ground in search of his expensive copper cable. He hulked through the front door, seconds from shifting.

The only being in the front office, a quaking receptionist, stammered, "C-c-can I help you, U-u-urso?" and didn't quite dive under her desk.

Sawyer put a flimsy lid on his wrath—this woman wasn't a fraction alpha enough to have created his problem. Poor little omega girl—if she went wolf right now she'd pee on the floor. She might anyway. "Tell me, how many spools of Milex 3 do you have on hand?" He settled his humanity more firmly—this wasn't who he'd come to bite. "Please."

She edged back into her chair and tapped digits into her computer. "Um... Seven. Where would you like them delivered? I'll schedule the truck..." She glanced up at Sawyer, and then her eyes widened, her gaze behind him. She exposed her throat submissively. "Lobo."

Rudy smelled of anger, covering the scent of his previous fear almost completely. If Sawyer hadn't known better, he'd have thought all the fear came from the young female. "Wolf," Rudy acknowledged her.

Sawyer had had enough of wolf pleasantries. "Seven, hmm. "On second thought, I might need DK 4. How much do you have of that?"

She snapped back to upright and typed again. "We have four of the big spools, Urso."

"Thank you...Lilly." Without the embroidered name on the left breast of her shirt, he'd not otherwise know. The pack grew bigger and bigger each year. And Rudy barely kept the wolves in line at the pack's lowest point. "Now pull up our last invoice and call your boss."

"Yes, Urso, right away, Urso." Her fingers flashed across the keys and the printer chattered. Before the paper sailed out into the tray, she lifted the phone. "Mr. Lowell, please come to the front office," boomed through loudspeaker in quavery tones.

A door opened, causing Rudy and Sawyer to turn.

"Lobo, Urso, what can I do for you?"

The last time Sawyer'd seen this man, he stood naked on the pine duff, arguing about hunting rights. Now Sawyer would hunt on his territory. "We're going to go count spools of heavy duty electrical cable, Brian."

CHAPTER THIRTEEN

Sawyer didn't wait for an answer, nor did Rudy. The Lobo's nemesis might crackle with fury, adding anger to the heavy scents of plastics, machine oil, and metals drifting in from the open warehouse door, but no matter how Brian might raise whatever pitiful hackles he had in human form, he dared not contest the two most alpha males in his world.

So Rudy's discipline held that far. Good. Rudy pushed Brian through the door into the high-ceilinged, chilly warehouse. "Let's go check your stock of Milex 3, Brian."

Sawyer would let Rudy deal with his subordinate, right up until the Lobo couldn't make his pack obey Sawyer in all the ways they were bound to obey. Perhaps contracts and theft were puny human things, but even as bear, Sawyer wanted those agreements held. Adding a warning chuff, he let Brian and Rudy lead him to spools of unpleasantly familiar chartreuse.

"Count them with me," Rudy growled. Good, he made Brian tot off cable out of force of personality. Sawyer restrained his shift—some of the men working there might not be wolves. One did a double take and flung his forklift into reverse, beeping as he fled. Another dropped his clipboard and crouched into defensive stance, knees bent, hands raised, head low and teeth bared. Sawyer lifted a lip at him—he stayed frozen in place.

"...three. I mean, three here. We took the rest to a job site." Brian kept his head down but the defiance in his voice make Sawyer's palm itch to clout him one. Preferably with claws, just for knowing on which job site they'd find the missing spools.

Brazen it out, would he? Sawyer rumbled, "Then you'll have your young lady pull the invoice when we get back."

A growl swirled through Rudy's throat. "Let's go see about the DK 4."

They ignored rows of reddish-orange cable, but strode after Brian and his leaking fear and anger scents to double-high, double deep rows of cable coated in a true green. Sawyer totted them by eye in a trice, but Rudy forced a verbal count. "Two high, two deep, two across. How many is that, Brian?"

"Eight." Brian stiffened his spine. "Exactly as it should be."

"Interesting, when your official inventory shows there should be seven spools of the lesser weight and four of the heavier cable." Rudy's voice went dangerously low, reverberating under the high ceiling.

The chill air in the warehouse should have dropped another ten degrees when Sawyer added, "And I have exactly four spools of what you're missing. Funny how that should be, Brian. Even funnier since I paid for the inventory you're showing long."

"You don't know squat about my inventory," Brian shot back. The fear leaking out of his pores didn't dampen his bravado.

"I know what you should have, what you do have, and what we have. And that there are forged labels on what you delivered," Rudy interrupted. "How are you going to make that right, Brian?"

"You signed for it, it's yours." Brian stood straighter, his arms slightly spread. "You want more cable, write a check."

Looking bigger didn't faze Sawyer: if he stood bigger he'd be three or four times Brian's size.

Didn't seem to bother Rudy either—he took a step closer to his mouthy challenger, somehow larger, definitely more threatening. "So you're fine with cheating your clients, not to mention your Lobo and your Urso?"

"You got a problem with me, write a review on Yelp." Brian took a step closer to Rudy, nearly chest to chest. "You're a shitty Lobo and wolves don't have an Urso. So get the fuck out of my warehouse."

"Formal challenge, Brian?" Rudy's ears grew pointed and furry, perking over the top of his head. "Right here, right now?" His next words garbled on their way out of his elongating snout. "Either make this right or issue challenge." Or get your ass whupped hung in the air.

Brian's gaze flicked between Rudy and Sawyer. Sawyer didn't even twitch: he'd leave wolf power struggles to the wolves. For now.

Damn it all, if Rudy had been training Jerry properly, he wouldn't be talking about challenges with no pack to back him up. Sawyer didn't trust the motley group of warehousemen, sniff, all wolves, gathering around them now, to choose the right side.

Brian was Rudy's problem. If any of the half dozen betas and gammas interfered, Sawyer'd be their problem. He caught their eyes and grumbled deep in his throat. Any smart ones would heed the warning. Didn't keep their eyes from growing bright with the bloodlust.

The wide aisle crackled with energy—if the cement underfoot wasn't the springy loam of a forest floor, it would still soak up shed blood. Rudy and Brian stood poised on the edge of violence, both staring into eyes gone yellow. The moment hung. Rudy waited, half man, half beast, for the still fully human Brian to decide if battle would come.

Sawyer could feel each pulse of their hearts in a time stretched to forever, heavy war drums thudding within their chests. His own pulsed in time with his ally's—if he could lend Rudy strength with each beat, he would. Brian was solid for a human, muscular and in the prime of his early thirties. In any battle while human, he'd have the advantage over a man fifteen years his senior and maybe a little softer around the middle. But as wolves?

More evenly matched as wolves, but for the pack. Were these wolves Rudy's pack? Or were they already Brian's, seduced by jobs or rhetoric? Would wondering take the heart out of Rudy? Or distract him? Would knowing they had his back give the challenger extra strength, or desperation to keep Rudy from punishing them?

Sawyer stood in the circle of wolves, where even the receptionist joined the ranks to see how the next few moments would play out. If he needed to be bear, he would, but... He couldn't fight Rudy's battle for him.

Sawyer would keep the battle Brian's alone.

Brian broke, his tension coming out in a snarl. "I call challenge, Rudy. You're old, you're soft, you've traded away our pack's sovereignty. I call challenge, Rudy; you're unfit to be Lobo."

Rudy snarled back. "I am experienced, I have made alliances to benefit us all. So I call bullshit, Brian. You've lied, you've stolen, you have no honor. You are unfit to lead a business, let alone the pack. You're unfit to issue challenge. You are unfit to be Lobo."

Sawyer wanted to smack his forehead. Every word Rudy spoke rang true, and only force could refute the truth. Brian could no more agree and back down than he could shift into a dragon. What did Rudy think he'd do? Cringe and say, "Yes, of course, Lobo, I'm a lying thief with delusions of grandeur and I'll go away now"?

Yet he might as well speak the truth—this battle became inevitable the first time Brian stood against Rudy and walked away unscathed.

Brian snarled, his face lengthening into a snout. "Lobo I will be!"

He reached for his shirt, but his hands had gone too far in their transformation to paws. He scrabbled at his clothing, trying to be free of the fabric hindrances. Rudy, faster, smarter, whipped his shirt over his head in hands still hands. Before Brian could react, Rudy'd flung his blue polo shirt over Brian's head, entangling him while Rudy finished his shift. He leaped free of his trousers, his tail fouling on the waistband only a moment, and became a snarling, slavering dervish.

Brian fought with the shirt wrapping his face and managed to escape his jeans, but not before he bled. Rudy snapped and connected, his teeth in Brian's flank. He shook his mighty head, the black fur of his ruff flying against the white background of the shirt Brian hadn't managed to remove before he went wolf. The cotton ripped, or was that flesh? Rudy knocked the other wolf to the ground.

Brian went down with a howl and came up, still wearing his shirt on his now furry torso, the buttons tight around his neck. He growled, head down, circling, meeting nothing but fangs. Yet he scored against Rudy, drawing blood with a savage slash on one leg.

The circle of wolves swayed inward, their heads down, still in human form. They stayed in place, though one man next to Sawyer reached to the hem of his work shirt. Sawyer clapped a meaty hand to the back of his neck. Gripped from behind, the man went limp like a puppy, his shirt in place.

Asserting dominance wolf-style worked, even for bears. Sawyer didn't let go.

The huge black wolf that was Sawyer's site supervisor in two-foot times struck and slashed, his lips drawn back in fearsome snarls when he wasn't using his teeth. Brian's white dress shirt grew red with blood, still choking him, hindering. A button flew from the neck and pinged against a shelving unit. Brian drew air in great gulps. His eyes brightened with each breath.

Rudy gave him no chance to recover. His furry blackness darted close in a flurry of snapping and a spray of gore. The gray wolf in the incongruous shirt went down, once, twice. Still he didn't yield, and even in his agonal howls his teeth closed on his opponent. Rudy's dark fur showed no stain, yet red splotches marred the gray cement.

The circled pack growled, whether for Rudy or for Brian, Sawyer knew not. Nor did he care. His combatants would finish their duel. If any wolf interfered, they would end yelping on the ground, not part of the battle. If he dared not let Brian's allies intervene, neither could he allow Rudy's faction a chance.

A growling male to Sawyer's left made to strip his work shirt away. With more of a will than a thought, Sawyer's left arm went huge and furry, his hand a padded paw armed with scimitars.

No sense in ripping his clothing when a partial shift would do. Sawyer slammed curved daggers into the interloper's belly. "Stay where you are."

Blood spurted from the would-be challenger—he folded double over Sawyer's massive paw.

His claws would stanch the wounds for now, all five of them.

The other wolves sucked in breath. They leaned back, taking themselves out of the fray. All but the receptionist, whose eyes rolled up into the back of her head. She crumpled to the concrete.

Sawyer hadn't a hand to come to her rescue. He'd immobilized two of the possible interferences and couldn't risk the others seizing an opportunity. Not when Rudy went down on his side beneath a gray fury.

Still Rudy's bright fangs did their bloody work. Even prone he snapped and connected, ripping both shirt and flesh along Brian's belly. His challenger squealed, toppling. Rudy dragged himself to his feet, his canines at Brian's throat. He growled, and Brian turned his face to the floor.

Shifting his muzzle alone, Rudy demanded, "Do you yield? Or must I kill you?"

For answer, the stone-gray wolf went limp.

Not as clear as words, but enough for Rudy. He pulled back, shifting into a bloodied figure of a man. Mature and commanding, he towered over his fallen challenger. "Brian, you are defeated. You live by my sufferance, though it is my right to kill you as you lay. My right. Perhaps my duty. Even if your Lobo is a sentimental fool, still I would let you live. If you yield."

If the gray wolf collapsed any further, he'd be a rug. Brian's sides barely lifted with his breath.

Crackling with wildness, Rudy surveyed the circle of wolves. "My challenger lies defeated. Would any take his place?"

No one answered.

Even Sawyer felt the power radiating off the Lobo. He forced himself to return stare for stare, authority for authority. Rudy's command would be enough now—Sawyer released the wolf he held by the scruff and let his massively clawed paw return to a muscular forearm with blood slimed beneath his nails. The wolf he'd stabbed into stillness collapsed to the cement.

No one answered Rudy's provocation. Those who remained upright turned their eyes away. Submission. Rudy had earned their obedience.

"Remember this. Remember who is your Lobo. Remember what mercy is, when you wake tomorrow as a living wolf." Rudy jerked his thumb at his fallen opponent. "Heal him. And when he's healed, remind him you all live by my mercy. And ask yourself, if the victory had gone the other way, would he have shown my loyal wolves the same?"

Rudy bent long enough to sweep his clothing from the floor. More blood gushed from his wounds. Not bothering to dress, he swung his stare around the frozen circle of wolves. "There will be four spools of the correct cable delivered to my job site by three this afternoon. No charge. No exchange. And no further cheating."

"Yes, Lobo," came in a low chorus tinged by shame.

Rudy marched out, leaving his wolves behind. Sawyer fell into step beside this unusually commanding presence. How had Brian even thought to challenge a Lobo like this?

Oh, because Rudy wasn't usually like this, not even a glimmer.

Rudy swung into the passenger seat, slamming his door even while Sawyer went around to the driver's side. He pulled out into the street, and before they reached the ramp to the highway, Rudy collapsed against the rich leather, his chiseled face gone pale. He jammed his shirt against the mangled flesh where his neck met his shoulder.

Sawyer caught the motion. "Why aren't you shifting?"

"Too weak," Rudy gasped.

"How do I help?" Sawyer knew exactly how he'd help a bear to shift, but even in a vehicle the size of the Escalade there wouldn't be room. And would his methods work on a wolf without causing further damage?

"Need the pack. But not them." Rudy's head lolled. "Can't show weakness. Not near Brian."

"Where do we go?" Sawyer demanded. He knew where he'd take Rudy, but it was so far. Up into the mountains. Did Rudy have allies closer to hand?

Did it matter? Rudy couldn't tell him anyway—his head flopped alarmingly and his hand dropped from the makeshift dressing. The polo shirt fell away from the torn flesh. Blood dripped in fat, red trails down Rudy's chest to soak the jeans lying in his lap. The copper-penny scent filled the big SUV.

Sawyer hit the gas. The Escalade zoomed west up the highway. To the mountains.

CHAPTER FOURTEEN

His first office visit hadn't left Dillon enthralled with the medical system, and his three weekly visits so far with the nurse practitioner hadn't left him any happier to be poked, prodded, measured, or otherwise investigated. Margo Frost seemed nice enough—all matter of fact about his condition, though he suspected her of having hysterics privately over the whole thing.

Moon knew he'd had his share of demented laughter and burning tears. Crying all over his buddies at the house was only the start. How had his life gone from amazing with a lover to lonely nights alone with his starting-to-bulge belly and an assortment of furry forms draped over him. He could go join the friendly fray, but... He wanted Sawyer. Only Sawyer. To get frisky with, to cuddle with, to dream about their cub's future with, to... To punch in his smug face for creating this fucked-up situation.

If only the face-punching wasn't his first reaction to Sawyer's texts or calls, he could tell Sawyer everything about his appointments and the strange changes in his body. His craving for mushrooms finally subsided to manageable levels, meaning he could forage as a bear without ripping every rotten log to smithereens. He could even stroll through the produce section at the market without diving at the displays to feed his face.

Or he could, if he was allowed back at the local market any time soon. He had paid for everything he'd eaten, but after scarfing three of the big portabellas in front of two shocked little old ladies, he'd been escorted to the door with instructions not to return until he learned some manners.

Oh Moon, he would have to teach little Boo-Boo manners. Dillon put his face in his hands with a sigh to rattle the glassware down at the bar. Where he would need to head shortly, because there were limes to cut and coolers to stock. If Jerry, Kevin, and Brad would please, Moon, just finish already and let him get through the living room to the kitchen without having to field unwanted invitations or jokes that left Kevin and Jerry in stitches.

Brad didn't laugh, though. Last time Jerry'd cracked one of his tasteless gags about buttbabies, Brad nipped him hard enough to make him yelp. Then he'd shifted and leaped into Dillon's arms to sniffle into Dillon's neck. Not that Dillon minded cuddling, but fox-snot apologies were kind of gross.

Oh damn. He'd be wiping cub-snot soon enough.

And cub-butt. Oh hell, maybe he could let the little fella stay in bear form until he was big enough to housebreak, and then Boo-Boo could do all his shitting in the woods. Like a proper bear.

But not a very good human. Boo-Boo had to know both.

How was Dillon going to learn to be a proper father to his cub? Did Sawyer know any more than he did?

He was so not prepared for parenthood.

Well, he'd better get prepared. After what the nurse practitioner said this morning during his ultrasound, Dillon didn't have a lot of time. Certainly not six months, not even three. Maybe not even one month.

2

Dillon lay still under the gel and the wand. Margo scanned this way and that.

"What a busy little guy he is." Her wand bumped up and down, tossed by movements Dillon felt in places he didn't usually think about. She exclaimed, "Little Bear weighs close to two pounds already!"

No wonder his jeans didn't fit right. No wonder he could see a bump in his middle he'd hoped wouldn't appear for a long while yet. "Um, how far along does that make me?"

She patted his shoulder in a motherly way at odds with her early-thirties appearance: unlined face and a swish of chestnut hair hanging down her back in a ponytail. Guess it was a wolf tail. Dillon knew her by sight from the pack, but she'd never created any problems he or Sawyer had to deal with. Rudy wasn't the sharpest claw on the paw, but he hadn't said anything against her.

"Well, if you were human, you'd be twenty-seven, twenty-eight weeks. Around seventy percent of the way through." She helped him to sit up, which he hated, but his center of balance had gone somewhere unanticipated.

"So, how much longer?" And could someone please tell him how the hell to get this cub birthed?

Margo made a note in the chart. "Let's put it this way," she said, flicking her pen with a suddenly ominous click. "The baby's doubled in weight since last week. His growth is accelerating. Your raging appetite is fueling his needs, and you said you're getting hungry every few hours."

Dillon wished he could go two hours without getting hungry. The breakfast burrito he devoured on the way to his appointment wore off long ago. If he wasn't sitting on the edge of an exam table in his underwear, he'd be rummaging in his backpack for the second one. The smell tormented him. "So if I wasn't eating all the time, the baby would grow slower?"

That earned him a stern look. "If you're hungry, you eat. You do not stint the baby or yourself. Growing that little guy is hard on your system—you don't hold back on fuel!" She softened a little. "All that would do is pull reserves from you to him. Babies are greedy that way. If I see you with hollows in your cheeks, I'll march you to the deli counter myself! Got that?"

"Yes'm." She might not be an alpha in her pack, but her medical credentials made her fearsome. "I'll eat properly. I've been trying." He'd been eating everything in sight, mushrooms or not. Jerry'd learned to throw an extra burger on the grill every time he got an order at the bar, and so far, Dillon kept all of them from going to waste.

"Good. When your appetite drops off, you'll know it's close to time." She smiled brightly. "That's how it works with wolves, at least."

"Great." Dillon hoped she ignored the rumble in his guts that could be heard in the next building. "Any estimates on when, though?"

Margo fiddled with a graph in the chart, making marks here and there. "Hmm, based on your last few weeks, you're getting a time contraction of..."

Oh, he did not want to hear anything about "contractions."

"Well, if you go three more weeks at this rate, I'd be kind of surprised." Margo bounced her pen against the graph. "Little Bear is growing really fast."

He could go three more weeks without sex—if necessary. Did he have to? If Sawyer still wanted to... Maybe Sawyer wouldn't want to scare the baby, or Dillon, or... Nope, Sawyer made it abundantly clear he thought Dillon was sexier than ever all knocked up, or rather, before he'd started showing. Maybe Sawyer would see... Oh hell, no point worrying if he shouldn't be doing the deed—he'd made himself scarce. And how could he ask? The question hovered on the tip of his tongue.

And wouldn't come out. So he asked the next thing on his mind.

"Erm, is it still okay if I shift?" Going furry had happened more than once since the full moon, but now he worried. And there'd be another full moon in the not too distant future. Would he hurt the baby if he kept going bear?

"Oh, my goodness. I don't know!" Margo's eyes went big. "Wolves shift right up to term, but... Once birth is imminent, we can't. Not until after the baby's born."

But they were girl wolves and built for carrying young. Damn. One more problem yet to solve. "And still no idea of how?"

Visions of the little bear growing and growing with no way out haunted his nightmares. Last night the baby grew and grew, filling up everything inside Dillon's skin, until finally he was entirely filled up. His skin split and he molted, the current Dillon sloughing off to let this new person walk away from the shed husk ... He'd wakened in a cold sweat. Brad had wakened too, since his furry form got rolled to the foot of the bed when Dillon sat bolt upright. The fox licked Dillon's face until his breathing stabilized. He'd lied and said he'd gotten a foot cramp. Brad licked harder and finally curled up at Dillon's waist.

"Well, no, unless we schedule a surgical suite. That possum doctor might want to get his naked little tail up here, or you go there, for the next few weeks." She brightened. "But something could come up! You never know!"

Depending on luck and "something to come up" sounded like the worst plan ever. "I'll call him."

"I'd have my primary doc do it, because I can't." That smile meant she already knew what she'd say next wouldn't work. "I just can't promise he wouldn't write it up."

Well of course not. If Dillon wanted immortality in the medical journals, he'd found the perfect way. He'd be right there next to Henrietta Lacks, and just as unhappy about making medical history. Damn. "Maybe I should buy a plane ticket."

"Maybe." She offered a small smile. "What if we installed a zipper?"

He dutifully laughed at her pitiful joke, but without real mirth. He'd have to talk to Sawyer. His bear promised he'd let nothing bad happen, so he'd better get his furry butt in gear.

Might be time to wear sweatpants to work. Dillon could either buy some new clothing or sling his britches way down low and let his "dunlap" hang over. So far no one outside his little group had twigged to his gut being anything other than beer, but he'd gotten a couple of pointed comments at the bar about laying off his wares.

Of course, the belly made a good prop for his textbooks when he read, but kept him farther from the kitchen table when he sat by a sunny window to study. Shouldn't have left his books behind when he'd moved out for what he thought would be a couple of days.

The phone call should have been simple enough, a quick, "Would you please bring my books by the house or the bar when you head into town?"

But no, Sawyer had to question him. "What for?"

Wasn't it obvious? "I need to study."

"Why?"

How could one bear get so many unwarranted assumptions into a single word? "Do you really think I'd drop my classes because of this... this accident of biology?" Dillon roared. "My brain did not disappear!"

If Sawyer hadn't realized the depth of his fuck-up, he would have reamed Dillon a fresh asshole for speaking so to the Urso. Instead, he appeared at the door that evening with a stack of books and a complete pot roast dinner. "I'm sorry."

A promising start, immediately screwed up. "I just thought you'd cut back. Maybe let Jerry and Kevin buy out your share of the bar."

"I'm doing the gestating here, Sawyer." Dillon snatched the texts and the fragrant food out of Sawyer's paws. "Your turn to make some sacrifices. You can be a stay at home dad as well as I can."

If Sawyer's eyebrows had risen any higher, they'd achieve orbit. Bet he hadn't even considered that.

Dillon didn't invite Sawyer in to share the meal.

Nor had he been inclined to share much of anything for

the next several weeks, beyond terse texts and the occasional phone call to inform Sawyer about his prenatal visits. And he still needed to get dressed.

Fuck it. He went for the low-slung look topped with a red T-shirt Sawyer'd left behind. His own weren't covering nearly enough. Dillon was debating a hoodie when the front door burst open.

"What the hell?" Willing himself not to shift, Dillon pelted toward the intruders ready to kick ass and take names. What if pitchfork-wielding crazies burst in who'd condemn his friends for playing in a great big pile of male horniness?

He rounded the corner to find his friends on their feet, with various drips and hickeys and the couch much the worse for wear. Much worse—another naked man lay bleeding all over the upholstery, and someone—Sawyer!—stood over him giving directions.

"Kevin, pick him up from behind. Body to body, yeah, that's right. Now Jerry, plaster against his front. Hand on the wound, yeah, I don't fucking care he's bleeding, just do it. Now!" Sawyer snarled, dragging his buddies into place. "He can't shift alone right now. You have to force him!"

"But I don't know how!" Jerry protested, though he did as he was told.

"Rudy hasn't taught you that yet?" Sawyer growled.

"Well, no, not exactly, but..."

"Can you feel him, feel his wolf-self?" Sawyer demanded. "It's like shielding, only the other way. Like you're trying to find him in spite of his shielding. Close your eyes and open your senses."

"I... I think I feel him." Jerry swayed on the spot. The man's head lolled alarmingly over Jerry's shoulder.

Oh my God! Rudy? What happened to the Lobo? Dillon stopped short. Brad stepped back uncertainly, bumping into Dillon. By reflex, Dillon embraced Brad, who turned and buried his face into Dillon's armpit. The little redhead shook—Dillon held tighter.

"Okay, good." Sawyer wrapped his massive arms around the three of them. "Pull him out of hiding. Demand he be here, present, as wolf. Grab him!"

Whatever grabbing Jerry did must've been metaphysical. Maybe Sawyer grabbed too: his face went tense, the muscles in his jaw clenched. The scar he'd never healed completely went white against his ruddy cheek. Sawyer clasped the three wolves in his mighty embrace, doing... Whatever would keep Rudy going.

Sawyer went to his knees, his arms abruptly full of wolves. Three of them, one buff, one sable, and one black. The black wolf rose to his feet, unsteadily, blinking against the light.

The other two wolves licked Rudy's face, cleaning him, feeling his life. Sawyer let go. "See how you do that, Jerry?" He stayed on his knees, his face at wolf-eye level. "Find the essence and pull. Pull him right out of his human form. Only the strongest can do that. You can, now that you know how. Rudy can, I've seen him. I don't think Brian can. I'm pretty sure Brian wouldn't try."

Rudy stuck his snout in Sawyer's face and licked his nose. "Yuck!" Sawyer laughed, one of those not happy, more relieved laughs, and fended him off. "How the hell do you shift with dog breath?"

Brad squeezed Dillon and turned around. "Um, are you guys hungry?" He flitted toward the kitchen with white buns flashing, reappearing with his hands full of lunch meat.

Rudy dove at the bologna, biting the wrapper in two just the way he'd get at steamy moose innards. The pink meat-ish stuff disappeared down his gullet in a few gulps. Jerry and Kevin kept back—stealing a bite looked like a quick way to lose a nose. Brad ran for more when Rudy gave him a green-eyed demand.

"What happened?" Dillon finally asked.

"Brian happened," Sawyer said absently, running his hands through Rudy's fur, searching for the places that made him flinch and finding a few. He rose, exposing the bloody smears on his clothing from Rudy's mangled human body. "We confronted him about a cheating problem. We may or may not be short a wolf. I don't think he was as badly hurt, or—" He favored Rudy, now gnawing hunks off a slab of cheddar cheese, with a sour glare. "—as stubborn about accepting help. But he went down, stayed down, and I think he's done as a challenger." Sawyer peeled his bloody shirt off, exposing his broad, furry chest.

Weeks of his own damn stubbornness seemed like major stupidity—Dillon could have been plastered against that chest, groin to groin with his mate.

Sawyer paused two steps away from Dillon. With his arms half out, and eagerness, or fear? He stopped short of embracing Dillon. "Are we—? Can I—?"

Dillon reached for his mate. His strong, loving mate, who'd saved the Lobo of the Ballantine Mountain pack. Dillon reached back. Sawyer wasn't merely a handsome, sexy, alpha bear and his Urso. Sawyer was the best damned thing on two feet or four, and Dillon was a fool to hesitate.

"Yes."

Sawyer stepped into his arms, holding fast, his mouth a dancing mess of lips and tongue. Dillon followed where he could, led where he couldn't, and tried to soak up the feel of his mate with every particle of his being. How could he stay mad at his bear? His wonderful, marvelous bear, who had a deep connection to his soul. The nights without Sawyer were a special kind of hell, and he'd cast his own self in.

"I missed you so much," Sawyer gasped. "So much. And our cub…"

Whoa. Yeah. Cub. That's why Dillon had been so pissy.

But Sawyer had a right to know.

"He's fine. Getting big." Dillon turned slightly sideways to place Sawyer's huge mitt against the bulge in his belly. Little Boo-Boo kicked away in there. Dillon still didn't know what to think of getting his pancreas tap-danced on, but he'd share the wonder with his cub's other father.

"Already?" Sawyer's brown eyes got huge.

"Yeah." Dillon longed to tell Sawyer the rest, but saying the words made everything too real.

"Um, Sawyer?" Jerry asked.

The living room was back to being full of naked guys and one black wolf snuffling the crumbs of cheese out of the carpet and favoring one paw on the previously chewed shoulder.

"What else should we do with him?" Jerry asked. "To get him all healed?"

Sawyer pursed his lips in a hmm. "He'll stay wolf for a while. Take him outside and help him catch something, and when he shifts back to human, he should be fine, or fine enough. He'll shift again if he needs to. Oh, and rub salt and vinegar into the bloodstains and run them through the wash."

"Okay. Sounds good." Jerry shifted back to four foot, nosed the screen door open, and led Rudy and Kevin out the back.

Brad started gathering up the bloody clothing. "Should I wash your shirt too, Urso?"

"Yes, thanks." Sawyer turned back to Dillon with hunger in his eyes. "I won't need it for a while." He reached back to continue their smoochfest.

Dillon hated to throw cold water on his mate, but... "Stop by the bar when the laundry's done, okay?"

Sawyer did a double take. "Wait, what? The bedroom's thataway!"

Dillon rasped his stubbly face across Sawyer's cheek. "I know. I also know that two of my co-owners are out running your problem wolf through the woods, and the third's trying to follow your orders. We have a business to run, and I'm the only one left to do it." A variation on the problem he'd been faced with the last time he and Sawyer saw each other.

"Let's send Brad down to open the bar and you and I can mind the laundry." Sawyer emphasized how little attention the washer would get by lifting his brows.

Dillon sighed. "That way lies disaster. Brad's too easy to distract. The customers would be drinking the top-shelf booze straight from the bottle while he's at the pool table, or on it. I have to be there."

And even if he didn't, Dillon wasn't ready for a trip to the bedroom. Everything was still too damned complicated. Sawyer didn't understand half of the concerns twisting around in Dillon's brain. And neither did Dillon.

And now with Sawyer up close and horny, Dillon had a fresh set of problems. Could Boo-Boo get a faceful of jizz? Would sex harm the baby? Would he remember? Margo hadn't said a word about fetal memories. But then, Dillon hadn't managed to ask the right questions.

"But—" Sawyer started to argue and stopped himself fast. That big breath had to be for calming enough not to debate himself into a "Yes, Urso, no, Urso, anything you say..." kind of situation. Or a "bellowing Arth" situation. The big bear was learning. "Yeah. I will."

"I'll even burn you a burger, and you can tell me all about what happened, and I can tell you more about Boo-Boo." Dillon made small amends, and maybe stirred up some fear, by rubbing Sawyer's hand against the undulating surface of his middle. Little cub was a dancing bear. The wonder chasing over Sawyer's face was precious. Dillon smiled. They were going to be daddies.

If Dillon survived.

❧

Letting Dillon walk out the door was so fucking difficult Sawyer wanted to shift and rage. They were on belly-rubbing terms again, and he left! Kisses and cuddles, and then nothing.

Nothing except a promise of a meal together and talking and all the clothes-on stuff he'd missed as much as the sex. And maybe Dillon shouldn't be a busy guy in the sack. Not in his delicate condition.

Sawyer dug a can of cola out of the fridge, snorting at himself. Dillon was hardly delicate: he was a bear shifter, tough as they came.

But what about the strange, fragile life he carried within? Their cub had pushed and stretched under Sawyer's touch. Dillon lived with constant reminders of the life inside him. Maybe... Dillon was right to be worried. But little Boo-Boo seemed so strong, bouncing his daddy's hand off with a kick.

Maybe, instead of sex, he should've mentioned the nursery, how he'd lovingly made the crib, and lathed pieces to turn into a rocking bear. Prove himself a good mate, worthy of the honor Dillon bestowed on him.

Sawyer wiped Rudy's blood and other dried substances off the leather couch. Nothing like a hide for resilience. He sat down to sip his drink and contemplate how to rebuild his and Dillon's bond with the addition of their cub.

Brad returned, washed and dressed. His freckles stood out against the paleness of his skin, and his shock of red hair looked like he'd finger combed after his shower. "Sawyer—"

"Sit down, Brad." Sawyer patted the couch, the only seating not currently overturned. Dillon's buddies certainly had been having a lively morning.

Had Dillon?

No. One whiff of Dillon's roommates reassured him Dillon hadn't been friendly with any of them, except maybe Brad, whose scent Dillon carried nearly permanently, but not in a sexual way.

Brad plopped onto the middle cushion and hesitated only a moment before leaning into Sawyer's side. "We like having Dillon back, but... You probably don't like that so much. Neither does he. He misses you."

Aw. Sawyer pulled the fox shifter into a one-armed embrace. Horny as foxes usually were, Brad seemed subdued. Worried. Maybe having one muscular arm smushing him into Sawyer's armpit would reassure him. Brad tensed and then went limp as a pelt. He sighed, his arm across Sawyer's bare stomach. Sawyer sipped his drink, patting the fox absently.

"I miss him too." Hell, Sawyer never thought he'd get so

into having a family, even one as motley as the one Dillon created with two stray wolves and an orphaned fox. And now he'd become the outcast. Jerry, Kevin, and Brad saw Dillon every day, kept track of his diet and heard his worries. Not Sawyer, his mate, the father of their cub. Not to mention all the antics this bunch indulged in that left the furniture askew. "I miss all you guys."

"We miss you too. And Dillon doesn't play with us. We invite him, but he just pats his tummy and says no thanks." Brad wrinkled his brows. "I don't know why."

Monogamy would be a foreign concept to a fox. Blow jobs weren't much different than nose-licks to them. Sawyer understood just fine. He understood even better now that Dillon carried their cub. Not that he'd played without Dillon before, no matter who else was involved. But now? Anyone who touched his mate would get bit, and not in the fun way. "I haven't been playing with anyone either."

Brad popped up, his eyes wide with alarm. "Oh that's terrible! Rudy and Eric haven't been taking care of you? We should have come up to the cabin, or down to your house, or..." He scrabbled at Sawyer's zipper. "You must be so deprived! I'll blow you right now!"

"No, no, it's all right." Sawyer captured Brad's slender wrists in his massive paw. "It's my choice. It's me missing Dillon."

"But—!" Brad's mouth hung open with the enormity. "Aren't you miserable?"

No, a fox wouldn't understand. Sawyer's misery wasn't orgasm deprivation, but Dillon deprivation. "Not in any way that you blowing me would fix."

Brad's chin quivered. Oops!

"You're sweet to offer and you're damned good at it." Better: Brad's chin stilled. "But until Dillon wants to play with me again, I'll manage." Sawyer stroked the side of the fox's head, trying to reassure him that this foreign condition of celibacy, however temporary, was survivable.

"But, he won't play with us and you won't play with us, and you guys won't play with each other! Are you ever going to play with us again?" Brad talked himself into near tears. "I thought we were family!"

"We are." Why had Sawyer thought uniting all the shifters on his mountain under his leadership was a good idea? He'd certainly never envisioned conversations like this when he'd laid down his law. "Families do more than fuck, Brad. They support each other, and help each other. You're supporting Dillon, even without sex, and so you're supporting me too. And even if I hate it, right now I have to support Dillon by respecting his boundaries. And I do hate it, Brad. I hate it so much."

The admission popped out of Sawyer's mouth, the words becoming reality before he could stifle them. Tears prickled in his eyes, threatening to roll down his face in a torrent. Damn, the Urso couldn't cry!

But right now, he wasn't the Urso: he was a confused and lonely bear.

With a member of the family he'd created diving hard into his arms. "O...okay. But I'll blow you if you want, you don't have to blow me back."

Brad must be very worried to offer such a concession. Sawyer almost chuckled, but he wouldn't hurt his little fox. "Thank you, Brad. It's just, you aren't Dillon. Can you save it for... for when we all play together again?"

If the day ever came. If Dillon would come to his bed again and fuck him senseless and then lie in Sawyer's arms to drowse.

Sawyer clutched the worried fox and felt him hug back, and then Sawyer cried tears of despair into damp red hair.

🖋

One of the lights over the pool table in the corner flickered. Have to do something about the tetchy bulb before the strobe effect drove patrons crazy. Anyone who didn't have a seizure would think he'd drunk his limit and stop buying beer. Bad for business. One of the ten thousand tasks a bar owner needed to do. Maybe this year's hibernation time had been good for his buddies, letting them learn how much really needed doing. Dare he hope he'd only have to do his 2500 tasks and not theirs?

Dillon dumped his slices of lime into the cooler, ready for the cases of Corona chilling in the walk-in. His concession to the hidden life pooching out his middle was to use the hand truck to haul the beer rather than pick up three cases at a time. Not that he couldn't sling sixty pounds like feathers, but he'd either not see where he was going or squish Boo-Boo.

He and Sawyer would have to choose their positions carefully, or they'd squish Boo-Boo into one flat little bear. How did women manage? They must: not a one of his nieces and nephews were flat.

He'd come so close to saying to hell with it and leading Sawyer to the nearest bed. And he would—soon. He couldn't stay mad forever; done was done, and all in good faith. Sawyer hadn't put a cub into Dillon on purpose.

133

This time.

But, now that he knew male bears could conceive... Dillon broke three glasses imagining a next time.

CHAPTER FIFTEEN

The bar rang with juke-box odes to cheatin' wimmin and broke-down trucks, and men's voices debating whether the Cubs could do it again. Of course they could: cubs could do anything, and Sawyer would help Dillon raise theirs to be strong and smart.

Oh, baseball. Well.

Sawyer pushed through the wall of honest sweat, beer, and browning hamburger fugging the Bear Claw even this early in the evening. The other men might not recognize him for who he was, but they opened a path for him, all the way to the bar. Dillon presided there, pulling pitchers of draft and dealing cocktail napkins like cards.

Sawyer watched him work, listening to the banter he exchanged with the customers. He was in his element, making everyone welcome and happy. Even Sawyer, even at a distance, because he admired a master at work.

Less than a year ago he'd strolled through the bear-clawed doorframe in search of unknown shifters encroaching on his lands, and he'd found...everything he never realized he needed.

He shifted his gaze to the pool table in back, where he'd gotten his first taste of his mate, and made a discreet package adjustment. Damn how fast the memory of sex with Dillon hardened his cock.

He'd no idea the night he'd roared up on his Harley the impact the next few hours would have on his life. Yeah, he'd found the stray shifters, all right.

And they weren't stray anymore. They belonged. He belonged.

Finally Sawyer took the last few steps to the bar, knowing he wasn't coming as a surprise—he'd seen Dillon's nose twitch. The place had to smell hideous to a bear with hormonally enhanced senses. At least Sawyer would have to get closer to the guys at the pool table to know what aftershave they used.

"Heya!" Dillon greeted him with a stein of something golden and hoppy. The cool drink almost made a good substitute for a hello kiss in this public place. Sawyer lifted his mug in salute, and with nothing but a raised eyebrow, cleared a seat at the bar. The previous occupant nearly left his drink behind in his haste to vacate the premises. Sawyer called him back— he reached for his glass as if Sawyer might take the hand off for daring.

"Got all the stains out," Dillon observed, his hands busy with levers and hoses.

"Brad gives good laundry." Sawyer toasted his little buddy with a sip. Or perhaps he was applauding the slight wince at his phrasing. "And Rudy had a nice long romp in the woods. Hope you weren't saving that chunk of elk for a special occasion."

"Only dinner tomorrow," Dillon growled. The rumble cut off like a switch—he must have considered the reason behind Rudy's ravenous appetite. "How's he doing?"

Good: Dillon remembered his position as Arth of Ballantine Mountain. "Fine and dandy. Now. Were you going to burn my burger personally? And do you want one?" Sawyer winked. "I know the owner. He might let you have a few minutes off to eat."

For an answer, Dillon shouted a request through the hatchway. He called twice more before Jerry responded. He'd ridden with Sawyer and could have been at the grill already, but the guy took his time getting out of the truck and into the kitchen. Brad pattered by with a tray of empties. Hmm. One empty. And there were dirty tables.

Dillon called the fox's attention to the problem with a quick aside. He scurried to obey, and got two tables cleared before getting distracted by the action at the pool table.

"Brad," Dillon growled, just loud enough to make the fox set down the blue chalk and hand the cue to the tatted biker he'd borrowed it from. "He's still not used to how much busier we are since I've come back."

Guess Dillon had his hands fuller than Sawyer thought. Last time he'd walked into this bar, he'd indulged himself in an after-closing blowjob with the bear who'd become his mate, and hadn't given much thought to how the place stayed open.

Might have been a grim winter around here, without Dillon to ride herd on them.

Not something he could discuss with Dillon here and now. Not his business, either, aside from involving his mate.

Paw-ternity leave might be a problem too.

Kevin took over at the bar when bringing the burgers, piled high with sautéed mushrooms steaming under a melted layer of Swiss cheese, through the hatch. Dillon grabbed both plates and motioned to Sawyer to follow. Wonder how long it would take some brave soul to sit down in his vacated chair?

"Glad everything worked out." Dillon set the plates down on the scratched wooden desk in what passed for an office in the back room. The piles of paper took up most of the surface—Dillon pushed them aside. He pulled another chair up to the desk.

The single-minded intensity with which Dillon pounced on his chow worried Sawyer. Dillon wolfed his burger and started on the fries before Sawyer'd finished his second bite. "When did you last eat?"

Dillon paused with three fries hovering near his mouth. "A couple of hours ago. Roast beef sandwich and an apple. Why?"

"You're chowing down like it's been days since your last meal." Sawyer was ready to shake Jerry and Kevin for letting Dillon neglect himself, but he also knew how Dillon built his sandwiches: one millimeter shorter than the widest he could open his mouth.

"Feels like it." Dillon chomped at the potatoes like they might escape before he could devour them. "It's been like this for the last couple of weeks. The bigger Boo-Boo gets, the more ravenous I get. The nurse practitioner says it's normal. By the way, I gave her your number for emergencies."

As Dillon's mate and Urso, and Boo-Boo's daddy, of course Sawyer should be called first. Even if Jerry or Kevin might get there faster.

"How is Boo-Boo?" Sawyer held his breath. Dillon was discussing pregnancy-related things calmly, like he'd accepted the situation as real and okay and not a reason to claw down whole forests in frustration.

"Doing good. Busy. I think he likes music. He starts kicking really hard when the Beastie Boys comes on the jukebox."

The hand not currently snagging the last of the fries cupped protectively around the bump in Dillon's middle.

Sawyer's heart hitched in his chest. Their cub, having opinions even from the dark haven of Dillon's insides, doing things Sawyer couldn't share. Because his mate needed space.

"He's doing it now."

His food forgotten, Sawyer slid to his knees at Dillon's feet. With a question in his eyes, he slipped his hands beneath the red cotton, cupping the swelling of Dillon's middle. Cub feet or cub hands pushed out against his palm. "Oh," Sawyer breathed. "He is."

The only thing more wonderful than feeling their son move was feeling Dillon wrapping his arms around Sawyer's shoulders while their son moved.

He could kneel here forever, or until Dillon was ready to give birth, or until he got hungry again... But just to feel the new life they'd made together. Dipping his head brought his lips to Dillon's skin. Little baby punches wouldn't hurt at all, no they were a sign of the strength of their growing cub. He bathed Dillon's bulge in kisses, willing them through his mate's body to their son.

"You're a thin layer of skin stretched over a thick layer of muscle, with the world's most active bowling ball inside." Sawyer laid his cheek against Dillon's bulge.

"He feels like the world's most active bowling ball. Little guy does the liverdance half the night. When he's not doing the bladder dance." Dillon winced. "It is very, very strange not to be alone inside my own skin, you know?"

No, Sawyer didn't know, but he wanted Dillon to tell him. To share the wonder and the joy of their cub. Why, oh why, couldn't Dillon have stayed these last few weeks? They could have moved down to Sawyer's city home, where Liza would be thrilled to whip up a new snack every few hours and Sawyer could spend his evenings leaning against Dillon's middle. Feeling their son grow. Speaking of which— "How much longer?"

Whoa, did Dillon just turn to ice? "Not long, maybe two-three weeks. And I still don't know how."

Sawyer'd do anything to bring back the moment. "Want me to drag Dr. Livingston by the scruff of his neck? Or no, I could make him shift and bring him back in a pet carrier!"

"Very funny, Sawyer." Dillon stood up, gathering plates. He stepped away, holding the dinnerware like a shield in front of him. "Make sure he packs his medical bag first."

Dillon left Sawyer alone in the back room, clutching the tatters of what could have been. They could have kissed, they could have dropped trou and had lovely make-up sex right there on the desk. Sawyer'd been seconds away from reaching for Dillon's zipper. He could have licked Dillon to full erection, blown him there with his forehead pressed against the baby-bulge.

Ugh, sounded a little weird when he thought about it like that.

Damn it! If Sawyer wanted Dillon back, he'd better get cracking on this "how to deliver their baby safely" thing.

CHAPTER SIXTEEN

Not looking at his belly didn't make his problem go away.
Well, his offspring, but until little Boo-Boo lay safely in
Dillon's arms, he presented a problem. Turning sideways
to the steamy mirror, Dillon forced himself to look, really
look, at his naked form. If he wanted to see his dick, he
needed a mirror. Even erect, a seldom event these days.
Peeing created another issue, working best if he pretended
to whizz in the dark. Otherwise he'd look down at his dick
in his hand and see nothing but baby bump, and the fright
made him spatter.

And here he was, muscular and defined, with the lightly
furry pelt covering his chest and arms. Just like always, except
for the rounded expansion that left his belly button stretched
into an oval. Dillon gave himself a critical once over. Would
Sawyer still want him?

Well, maybe there wouldn't be any permanent changes,
although his treasure trail had widened. Hmm, maybe? But
no, Dillon's questing fingertips found nothing but body hair
there, no sign of a developing way to expel his parasite. Um,
child. Cub.

He rested his hands against the Boo-Boo-bump. Dillon
wanted to love his child—he'd be a good father—if he stayed

alive! While Dillon was capable of taking a mighty cock like Sawyer's balls deep in his ass, there was no way something the size of a baby could come the other direction. If Kevin made one more assbaby joke, there would be blood on the floor! It wasn't funny, not when Dillon's ass lay on the line!

Maybe he'd better make plane reservations and get back to Possum Kingdom for the duration. Sawyer'd promised he'd let nothing bad happen, except Dillon wasn't seeing any action or answers. So he'd make his own.

He dressed in sweatpants and a T-shirt two sizes larger than he'd ever needed. Jerry's contribution to the pregnancy effort. Smartass wolf ordered one saying:

I'm pregnant
I'm uncomfortable
I'm grumpy
Were you about to say something?

When presented with the oversized garment, Dillon gave Jerry a look capable of curdling milk at thirty paces and exchanged the shirt for one marked:

How about a nice cup of shut the fuck up?

Two more weeks of this? He'd know more after his visit to the nurse practitioner this morning.

"Oh, my!" Margo exclaimed, eyes and mouth wide. "Four pounds of strong, healthy cub. Won't be long now. He'll soon be ready to make his entrance into the world."

"HOW?"

Dillon didn't think he'd ever be ready.

Dr. Livingston had proven a nut too tough to crack the last time Sawyer'd called—before they knew the nature of Dillon's condition.

The hold music played its seventh rendition of Pachelbel's Canon while Sawyer's temper flared. He'd taken to stabbing his pen into a stack of papers every time the violins hit the quick section, which wasn't doing his desk a bit of good.

He didn't need that bid sheet anyway.

Not as badly as he needed to make his case. So when the doctor finally picked up the phone, Sawyer managed to channel his snarls into "worried father gruffness," or what he hoped commanded enough respect to make his point without being overbearing. Damn, he needed to be diplomatic!

He could do diplomacy: hadn't Sawyer brought a mountain of warring shifters into some kind of cohesion, plus or minus a Brian or two? Easier when he could administer a swift smack, or a wang up the wazoo, but still, he was a man as well as a bear: he could use words.

"Doctor, I thought you'd like to know how Dillon's doing. Have you been in contact with Margo Frost?" There! Smooth! He'd even managed not to growl.

"It's an odd situation, really," Dr. Livingston replied. "He's not exactly my patient, but I haven't formally relinquished care, either. I shouldn't be indulging my curiosity if I'm not involved."

"Oh, I think you should indulge your curiosity as much as you like." Sawyer pounced on the opportunity. "Since Dillon's due within the next two weeks. And you're still formally his doctor. And since Margo can't perform abdominal surgery on her own. So wouldn't you like to bring your husband and son to Colorado for a vacation, at the Ballantine Sleuth's expense? Stay in a gorgeous mountain cabin with a hot tub and all the amenities?"

Sawyer even tried throwing his housekeeper Liza in as an enticement—"All your meals cooked on site by a pro"—but Dr. Livingston kept saying no.

"Sawyer, it's very enticing, but the fact remains that my secretary is due shortly, and she is indubitably my patient. I have a responsibility to her. Not to mention another member of my passel expecting quadruplets." Dr. Livingston sighed.

"But it's just after the full moon, and spring, the first crickets will be out," Sawyer wheedled, only to be shut down. Again.

"You're putting me in a terrible bind, Mr. Ballantine, but my first responsibility is closer to home." Dr. Livingston sounded grim but final. "You'll need to involve the nurse practitioner's primary, and risk the publicity. I'm sorry. I can't leave Tiffany and Mrs. Johnson to fend for themselves, even though they have, as you put it, standard birthing parts."

Sawyer's last "But—" got a quick interruption.

"Mr. Ballantine, I'm being called to an emergency. I have to go."

And Sawyer was left speaking to a dial tone. Damn possum could be quite the alpha when two thousand miles of distance prevented looming.

There had to be a plan B. There had to.

CHAPTER SEVENTEEN

Every seat in the living room was full this time, even the ragged brocade wing chair with the gnawed arm and the faint odor of wolf piss—his grandmother's favorite, and Brian never liked the old bitch. She'd said nasty things like "No" and "mind your manners, pup." She might be gone but her chair still got the occasional late revenge.

Brian's receptionist Lilly currently sat on the edge of the undesirable seat, because every cushion of the long couch and the loveseat contained someone more alpha to her. Even the ottoman had been claimed. Nobody dared sit in Brian's "throne" with the lift-up footrest.

The remnants of a pizza feast littered the floor, along with plenty of beer cans. Brian fed his band of wolves well. One day he'd sort out who showed out of cupboard love versus who showed out of allegiance, but for now, he wasn't taking any tally that diminished his numbers. Eight of his followers came tonight, though they may have mistaken a war council for a social event. Anyone with a loyalty based on appetite still needed to pull his or her weight.

And anyone who changed sides after the recent failed challenge wouldn't survive very long. Brian's next assault on Rudy would happen at a time and place of his choice and with planning. That challenge would see him the victor. And then there'd be a housecleaning.

Not all of his guests witnessed his humiliation. Those who hadn't asked too many damned questions.

"I was goaded into this challenge," Brian snarled. "And I would have won, too, except for that ragged old rug Sawyer Ballantine! Who the hell said he could interfere in the affairs of wolves?"

"Rudy did." TJ spoke around a half-chewed pizza crust.

Mark one cupboard love follower, and not too bright. Did he think Brian wanted an answer? "Rudy has no right to give our leadership to a bear! We're wolves! We're the pure wolves, who need no other animal to hold our rightful places. We have no need of a bear for our leader."

"He's not, not really. Mostly Rudy's ally," observed Carl, who clearly had no sense at all. After Sawyer had stuck curved claws into him, he still claimed the Urso wasn't trying to run things?

"And boss. He's boss to a lot of us, Brian." TJ peered into a pizza box in search of another slice.

"Then you damned well need to work for someone else!" Brian all but howled. He did not need this damned bear dividing the wolves with something as base as money. If Brian hired some dissatisfied wolves, he was only looking out for the welfare of the pack. Of course. "We don't need Sawyer fucking Ballantine! And we don't need Rudy!"

"Rudy did whup your ass," observed Josh. "So doesn't that mean you stop trying to take over?"

"No, damn it!" Brian shouted. He neither wanted nor needed to be reminded of a drubbing that had taken three shifts to heal. A week later and he still walked with a trace of a limp. "We have the same problems we had before, and there's no one else stepping up to the pump to take Rudy on. You were supposed to have my back, and where were you? Standing there with your thumbs up your asses because a bear said so! If you sorry dogs had jumped in like you were supposed to, I'd be Lobo now."

Lilly slid to the floor, hunched and exposing her throat.

No, his receptionist wasn't much of a combatant. "While you're down there, you can pick up the pizza boxes." Brian turned his attention to his more dominant followers. "Next time, and I assure you there will be a next time, you will jump in to help. And if you don't take on Rudy with me, you'll keep Sawyer off my back. Got that?" He stared directly into each set of eyes until the owner dropped their gaze. "We never had these kinds of problems before we had bears. It's all down to having a mountain infested with goddamned bears."

"Well, you're about to have more bears." Margo spoke absently, and damned if she didn't clam up fast.

"What? Why?" For fuck's sake, the last thing Brian needed: more bears!

But Margo wouldn't say a thing. Brian rose from his easy chair, bristling with every hair. He advanced on her, radiating his dominance. "Where are we getting more bears?"

It wasn't until he was snout to snout, erm, nose to nose, but close to shifting, with her that she spoke. She shrank deep into the couch cushions and in the tiniest voice possible said, "Sawyer's son."

Brian wanted to stand up straight and howl with laughter. "That big faggot, having a son? What's your next joke?"

So why wasn't she laughing with her "gotcha"? Nope, Margo stayed huddled down and reeking of fear. She said nothing. Brian repeated his question in a voice full of menace. "How is Sawyer Ballantine having a son, Margo?"

"Dillon," she whispered, her head turned to show her throat.

"Dillon is a man." Why did he have to state the obvious? He ought to rip her throat out for wasting his time with this crap!

"And he's pregnant." Margo cringed, never ceasing her submission.

Squinting her eyes shut only meant she wouldn't see him shifting for the kill. Disbelief came in more voices than Brian's. "How the hell is a man pregnant?"

"I don't know how. But he is." Margo whimpered, the puppy squeak begging for her safety, if not her life.

Brian might spare her if she kept answering questions. Bringing his teeth near her neck, he asked a question he could hardly believe could be answered. "How close is he to birthing?"

"Near term." She whimpered again.

Making a face likely to be stuck on "what the fuck?", Brian straightened up, leaving Margo unbloodied. "Fuck my life. More bears. More damned bears." The group stayed frozen, hunched up and not interfering while Brian paced the living room. He kicked a beer can out of the way and continued his mad whirl of frustration. "That's the last fucking thing I need is more bears."

"It's just a little one," Carl said. "Likely to be a distraction for the big ones. Then they'll stay out of our fur."

"It's little now, and then it gets big, and then it gets all up in our business, what with Sawyer teaching it to boss wolves. Fuck that noise," Brian snarled. His head hurt from trying to imagine a pregnant boar bear, but Margo was next thing to a doctor, and he could smell she wasn't lying. "And all the while, we got bears interfering, and keeping me from being the right-ful Lobo." He whirled and paced through the living room, cir-cuit after circuit.

Well, it was a hard thing, but a wolf had to do what a wolf had to do. Brian turned alpha laser eyes on the group. One at a time he held their attention, making sure no one formed any ideas of naysaying him. "We do not want bears. We do not need bears. We are getting rid of bears, starting with the unnatural faggot who got pregnant. We're going to take them all out, and then that mangy cur Rudy won't have anyone to stand between him and me."

"You want us to take on bears?" someone gasped.

"We start with the one who can't shift," Brian crowed. "If he's at term, or close, he's stuck on human. Easy meat, guys!" Wouldn't take much to whip his henchwolves into a killing frenzy—

"No, wait!" Margo yelped. "You're talking about killing the—"

Brian backhanded her right off the couch. She sprawled and lay still. Nobody else argued. Didn't think any of 'em would, even soft-hearted nursy-wursy, but the others showed the proper bloodlust.

"Hell yeah! Take out two thirds of the bears of Ballantine Mountain, and one of 'em can't even fight." Oh the more Brian thought about his plan, the better this sounded. "And that'll fuck up Sawyer so bad he can't think. Then we can take him. Come on, guys! Dillon'll be at the bar, and nobody else around!"

Brian's wolves thundered out the door. If they were any more anxious to attack, they'd be slavering like their wolven forms. Good boys, all of them, with bloodlust ruling. Those pussy bears were gonna be so much bearburger when Brian and his pack got through with them.

≥

Everyone bolted out to the vehicles, leaving Lilly alone in the kitchen. She'd slunk out with the empty pizza boxes when Brian told her to clean up, but he hadn't said anything about coming back, and so she hadn't. He scared her so much, she thought she'd wet the floor right there in front of everyone. The beer cans could wait until the coast was clear.

And the terrible things he said! If he wasn't her cousin, she wouldn't be here, even if he did give her a job when things were rough. Brian might be family but, but she didn't like him, and she didn't trust him, and oh, she'd been right not to trust him, and now he wanted to do terrible things. Poor Dillon! Lilly whimpered into her hands.

An answering moan from the living room drew her back. She crept through the doorway to see Margo lying on the carpet, a huge bruise blooming across her face. Oh, what had her awful cousin done?

Margo moaned again and lifted her hand to her face. She winced, and the wince made her wince.

"Are you okay?" Lilly asked. Stupid question—someone strong as Margo ought to get up and shift if something wasn't radically wrong.

"'S 'ro'en." Margo scrabbled at the zipper to her jeans.

"Oh! Broken!" Lilly took over, helping Margo strip. Her shirt had to come off over her head—Lilly wailed "Sorry!" louder than Margo moaned for the pain. But as quick as

Margo shed her clothes, she could shift. Lilly tugged at her underthings.

With a hissed exclamation Margo rolled to her side—and didn't shift.

"What are you waiting for?" Lilly cried.

"'all srrrrr," Margo hissed again, her hand against her face.

"I don't understand!" Tears of frustration and fear rolled down Lilly's face.

"'AL SRRRRR! A 'LLLLN!" Margo insisted. And then she couldn't insist any more—she shifted, going slender in the leg and long in the snout. She went from brunette to gray all over, with a plumy tail she wasn't waving.

"I still don't know what you want me to do!" Lilly wailed, still on her knees.

Margo sniffed in a way that was more nearly a hmph! She dove behind the couch, returning with her handbag. She dropped the bag at Lilly's knees. She looked expectant, like Lilly should know what to do. But... Okay, something in there... Lilly unzipped the bag and set it down.

Margo grabbed her handbag again, with a jaw, that—yay!—wasn't broken any more. And shook. She shook all her stuff all over the floor, dumping her lipstick and wallet and cell phone and breath mints and things all over. Dang! Lilly had more to clean up!

But—Margo nosed through her stuff, found what she wanted, and dropped her cell phone on Lilly's thighs.

Oh! "You want me to call Sawyer!" Lilly could weep with relief, but the heat in Margo's eye said pretty plainly *Cry and I'll give you something to cry about.*

"Okay! Okay!" She poked at the phone, scrolling to the Ds. No Dillon. And no idea of his last name. Hiccuping in fear, she tried the Ss. No Sawyer. "Wait what... Oh!" She fumbled to the Bs. The ringing took forever.

"Ballantine Construction, Sawyer speaking" fell on her ears like sweet music.

Lilly started to gabble out the whole story, all at once, knowing she wasn't making a lot of sense. Conscious of Margo's gimlet glare and Sawyer's confused, "Whoa. Stop. What about wolves?" finally brought her to a halt.

She started over. "Urso, Brian and a bunch of wolves want to attack Dillon! They're headed to the bar now!"

"Moon curse them!" Sawyer snarled. "How far do they have to go?" He barked other orders away from the phone, about *do this do that I'm leaving.*

"I don't know!" Lilly wailed. "They left about ten minutes ago from 10th and Garrison."

"Call Dillon! I'm on my way now!" Sawyer roared and hung up.

A good little omega, Lilly wanted to obey. But she couldn't, not until Margo shifted back and told her Dillon's last name. Sawyer would be so angry if something bad happened for the delay. And Brian would be so angry for the betrayal. She was so screw—oops. Lilly peed on Brian's carpet.

CHAPTER EIGHTEEN

The daily bar tasks never ended. Things at the Bear Claw were better now since he'd convinced his co-owners to clean up the night before instead of walking back into a mess that only got worse. The glasses were clean, the beer restocked, the ice machine full. Excellent, because Dillon was already tired, and the evening hadn't started yet. Now to make sure nobody could stick to the bathroom floors. Mopping was Kevin's task, but he did it more often if he was reminded.

Like a kid. He was raising three kids, dang it, they just looked like young men when they weren't furry.

His friends gave him lots of practice for raising Boo-Boo. Dillon ran a hand over his belly, swollen to the point of discomfort. Worse when the cub landed a direct hit on his bladder. He couldn't pass the men's room without taking a leak, which Kevin took as a slur on his mopping skills.

If ol' furrybutt would finish the impromptu shenanigans in the walk-in cooler so Jerry could pat out some burgers for tonight, he might get in here and do his job. Dillon made a face and zipped up. At least they had a half hour before switching the neon sign to "Open."

He waddled out of the men's room in time to see a group striding through the front door. Who was supposed to have locked up? Dammit, one more task he had to nag someone about.

"We're not open yet, gentlemen," Dillon called across the barroom.

The group, all men, and, sniff, wolves, marched through the tables and chairs, shoving the furniture aside.

"We're not here for the beer." The leader smiled toothily, might as well have a thin ribbon of tongue lolling out of his mouth already. "We're here just to see you, Dillon."

Brian. Fucking Brian. And his henchies, six of them, all with shit-eating grins.

"You're looking pretty good, considering how Rudy wiped up the floor with you last week." The best defense was a good offense, and Dillon planned to push the offensiveness. "Did you need two shifts to heal, or three?"

"Doesn't matter. Does it, boys?" Brian didn't even turn around. "Cause I'm here, and my wolves are here, and you seem to be all alone, Dillon. Isn't that special? Because we wanted to ask you some questions in private. Seeing as how you might be embarrassed by the answers."

"Out, Brian, and take your little pack with you." Dillon had no trouble looming—he stood a good four inches taller than the tallest of his opponents. Even his oversized shirt added to his bulk.

Nobody backed off. Dillon gave them hard eyes, calculating who might be brave enough to take another couple of steps farther, and which way he could fling the bodies to break the fewest barstools. He wouldn't shift unless forced, but the first wolf who went to peel down enough to go furry would regret the decision.

One enraged bear, seven werewolves. Guess Kevin would have to mop the whole barroom before they opened.

Might be kind of nice if Kevin and Jerry made an appearance. Jerry's power needed a live test. No time like the present. If Dillon had to fight as hard as he had to maintain control on a dry run, Jerry ought to have this bunch squatting and whining in no time flat.

Brad would have the sense to stay back—he was outmatched anyway this shook out, and would need protecting.

"Now why do you have to be like that?" Brian drawled. "Maybe we just came to give you some congratulations."

"Don't need any, thanks." Dillon softened not at all. Damn it, if his wolf buddies could finish fucking each other silly and get out here, this might end without any bloodshed. Dillon was too damned tired to want to go six rounds. Looming took more energy than it used to. "Go on now."

Brian took another step forward. So did his henchies.

"We hear you're expecting a little bundle of joy, buddy." Brian didn't look overjoyed. "Damned silly thing to happen to a man, now isn't it?"

"Would be if it happened." Dillon wouldn't give up one iota of information.

Not that he had to—all of them had their lips pulled back in a flehmen, sucking and tasting the air. If Liza and Brad could scent his pregnancy when Boo-Boo was the size of a grape, his cub'd be even easier to detect now when he weighed close to six pounds.

How'd Brian find out?

Fuck. The midwife. The wolf midwife.

Moon curse it, things were gonna get busy. Dillon pulled in a deep breath. Thank Moon he wore sweat pants today: he could be out them in a heartbeat. Although he didn't care right now if they survived his shift.

Because nothing mattered unless Boo-Boo survived. With seven wolves lined up like they were the Earps at the O-K Corral, with Dillon as Billy Clanton, either one of them surviving didn't seem near as certain as it had twenty minutes ago.

Hah.

These assholes faced Papa Bear. They weren't going to know what hit them.

CHAPTER NINETEEN

Brian shucked out of his shirt, the signal for his backup to do the same. Oh man, they were starting to shift, melting into their four-legged shapes.

Didn't matter—Dillon hauled his T-shirt over his head in a fast one-handed maneuver—he couldn't choke himself until the fabric gave way. He held the limp gray jersey before him, not that it would shield his bulge from anything except prying eyes. They didn't need to see how his cub pushed his belly out, stretching the ridges of his abs and doing funky things to his belly button. His shaggy pelt would hide the evidence.

Dillon let go, the way Sawyer taught him. Let his humanity flow away until only his bear-self, all six hundred pounds, remained.

Nothing happened.

Seven gray wolves stalked toward him. Heads down, teeth bared.

Dillon let go again, willing his fur to appear, and the heavy muscles of the grizzly he was. The grizzly he needed to be, with growling death approaching.

His claws grew. His palms became pads, his forearms thickened and grew heavy with fur.

Nothing past his elbows.

Dear Fullest Moon, death came for his cub, and he had nothing but a human body and his claws.

And his mind and his voice.

"Jerry!" Dillon bellowed. "Kevin! We got wolves!"

Brian rushed him, teeth bared. The rest rushed too, though others surged ahead of their leader to meet the claws of doom. Bet that wasn't an accident, letting his pack be the ones to bleed and die first.

Dillon swiped his massive paw across the fangs leaping at him. He connected, drawing lines of gore on a shaggy neck. He knocked the first wolf sideways, smashing three of its companions into the carefully tucked chairs and tables.

Four down, though most wouldn't stay down. Dillon shot backwards, protecting his back against the bar. He couldn't risk his balance.

Two massive paws, even tipped with five claws each as long as his finger, couldn't defend all sides at once. Dillon smacked down another wolf, but someone got in behind him, shredding his sweats and opening a gash in his thigh. Dillon swung again, and his attacker crashed into a table.

More wolves joined the fray—friends Dillon couldn't maul. Moon bless, Kevin and Jerry'd finally gotten their furry butts in gear! A cream-colored blur materialized by Dillon's side, spattered with the blood he'd drawn on the way. To his left, the sable wolf known as Jerry pinned a gray wolf by the throat.

Dillon slashed again, aiming for the eyes. No holds barred—if the pack got him down, he and his cub were goners. Who knew which wolf was Brian in this fray? Markings and scent offered no help—the maelstrom of fur boiled with hatred and every fang snapped against them.

A red streak caught Dillon's eye. Brad darted in at the back, snarling viciously. Brat was outmatched, outweighed five to one, he shouldn't be in this fight!

One of the attackers screeched. Whirling around, a wolf snapped at the red fox who'd dared sink teeth into his testicles. He spun, swinging the fox around and around in the fruitless effort to catch up with his own back end.

Brat sprang away, leaping lightly over the wolves and letting his pursuer try to follow. The wolf snapped after the red brush, but Brat danced up and over, bounding to the bar and up into the rafters.

Someone was safe, for a while.

But not Dillon. Kevin went down under two attackers and a third wolf crashed into him. Dillon staggered under the weight, shoving frantically to keep fangs from his throat. More teeth slashed at his belly. Why could they still fight? "Jerry, do the whammy!"

He felt the wave of power, but dilute. Enough to make the wolves hesitate. Enough to knock Brad out of the rafters with a sickening thump. Not enough to halt the fight by a long shot, and then Jerry went down under a tsunami of gray fur.

A wall of fangs came at him. Foul breath, eyes glowing with evil.

Pain—pain to be slashed away with scimitar claws he could barely wield with his human arms. Dillon slipped and went down hard. His head cracked against the bar and the mob closed in.

CHAPTER TWENTY

Moon blind it, if this idiot didn't get out of his way right now, Sawyer would drive the Escalade right over the top of the Fiat. Too many miles separated him from Dillon to put up with a fool only doing seventy.

Oh dear Moon, let him be in time!

Sawyer turned the big SUV up the secondary highway, throwing his heart across the miles to get to Dillon. He'd promised to keep anything bad from happening to Dillon, but he'd never envisioned this. The she-wolf's nearly incomprehensible story frightened him to the bone. Would this damned truck not go any faster?

He screeched into the Bear Claw's parking lot. Four vehicles, only one of them Dillon's. Mother Moon, let the others belong to old alkies and hungry tourists, not the wolves. But a quick sniff as he slammed the door told him: enemy.

He shed his clothing as he ran, losing shirt and shoes before he ever hit the door. If they'd so much as threatened Dillon...

Sawyer burst through the door, swapping the bright sunshine for the dimness, but he could see enough. A writhing, snarling mass stinking of blood, with Dillon in the middle.

Dillon went down. The wolves were upon him.

Sawyer shifted: one moment a man, then seven hundred pounds of livid grizzly. Fangs and claws and muscle surged to the snapping, growling fiends tearing at his mate. Sawyer covered the distance in a flash, barging through the tables. Nothing would keep him from Dillon.

Nothing would save those wolves.

He swung his mighty paw at the wolves. One crashed into furniture close to the door, another threw up his head to snarl and died from the claws slashing his jugular. Wolf after wolf went down in a spray of gore or flung across the room. Growls turned to squeals. Squeals turned to silence.

Brian kept his head down at Dillon's belly, torn open and bleeding. No! Not his mate! Not their cub! Sawyer's roar filled the bar and only then did the wolf turn to bare his teeth. His muzzle dripped with Dillon's life, and then he turned, jaws open, to the kicking, flailing form he'd exposed.

No! Sawyer slammed the wolf to the ground, his fangs in the murderer's throat. He ripped. Flesh tore. Blood sprayed, blinding Sawyer.

He ripped again and didn't need to see to feel how Brian died.

He rippled back into human form. Nothing mattered but Dillon, not even the two wolves flanking him, one with a shredded belly, the other's throat mangled.

"Dillon!" Sawyer roared, dropping to his knees beside the butchered body of his lover. He'd been in his lover's body, but not like this, where everything lay visible, including his diaphragm, still moving. Dillon lived, but only just.

And their cub! Sawyer snatched the baby up from his daddy's ruined body. The movement startled him. He began to cry, with the harsh squalls of a newborn.

"Dillon! Our cub! He needs you, you have to shift!" Oh fuck, he didn't have enough hands. What was he gonna do? Sawyer couldn't put their son down but he had to fix his mate. He had to! Scrabbling to put the important pieces back more or less where they belonged using only one hand, he begged Dillon to live.

A slight shadow fell across them: the fox stood on two feet. "Give me the baby, Sawyer." Brad took the newborn from Sawyer's grasp.

With both hands free, Sawyer could beg harder. "Shift, Dillon, you have to shift!" Sawyer gathered the limp body up, searching for the spark of life. He'd drag the very faint traces of his mate back, make him whole, if he could just find him.

Dillon moaned, a thin sound.

"Yes, yes, now shift!" Sawyer somehow had Dillon's life force now. But strain as he would, Dillon lay limp and human with his arms alone in the shape he needed. What kept Dillon from shifting?

Brad remained at his side, the baby as close as he could be. Should he try laying the baby on Dillon? Let the spark of their child call his daddy back from the shadows?

"Damn!" The cord! Their cub was born, but the cord binding their lives together remained inside the mutilated bear. It had been life for their cub, but their child could breathe for himself. And the cord still bound them, a foreign body now. Sawyer yanked on the cord, hand over hand, and hoped the only things coming out of Dillon were no longer needed. He flipped the damaged edges of flesh and muscle back into place and pulled again on Dillon's spark.

"Please, shift, Dillon. I love you." Sawyer gathered his wounded bear into his arms. So limp, so bloody. Still breathing, though his chest barely rose and fell. Tears fell into the gaping wounds. "I love you, Dillon. I need you. Our son needs you. Hear him? He's crying for his daddy, that's you. He's never been away from you, he hates it as much as I do. Shift, love, please shift!"

Dillon stirred, his paws flexing enough to scritch the barroom floor even through the puddles of blood. And then went still.

"You. Will. Shift!" Sawyer strove, with his entire being, with every scrap of his alphahood, for Dillon to take his rightful form. He'd promised nothing bad could happen to his lover, but he was foresworn. All he could do now was make sure the bad things weren't permanent. "Stay with us, Dillon! You can heal this. You're strong, you can! Our son is born, you have to see his face! Shift!"

He was Urso: he was strong. He could force the last scraps of Dillon's vitality to shift him and heal. He was Urso of Ballantine Mountain and his Arth would live!

And Dillon shifted.

Torn and broken became whole and furry. Still with red and furless seams, but the gory view of Dillon's internal organs disappeared under a coating of bloody fur. Too huge to stay in Sawyer's lap, too heavy even for the mighty thews of his arms, Dillon slithered down Sawyer's thighs to land on his back, all four paws waving in the air. He rolled and gained his feet. Slowly and painfully—this would be no "one shift and ready to run" recovery—Dillon stood up to snuffle Sawyer's face.

"Bear breath!" Huge tears rolled down Sawyer's cheeks. Dillon licked them away. But too soon, or, oh shit, maybe not soon enough, Dillon turned to whuffle at the fallen forms of the wolves who'd come to his defense. They lay still, too still.

Dillon lurched down, nearly covering Jerry's sable body. With a grunt of pain, he turned his massive head to call Sawyer to his side.

Sawyer came but— "There's no hope, Dillon. He's not gone but we can't force-shift wolves."

Dillon grumbled low in his throat. He bent his head, his eyes shut and nearly lost in the fur, trembling with his effort.

The baby screeched again, a sound to break Sawyer's last nerve. He should go to his son, but... Jerry had given his all for Dillon and their baby.

Sawyer lay down next to the bear and wolf, touching them both. "Let's do this!"

The effort was the same, the spark more elusive. Yet with Dillon's strength, low though it was, they found the essence of their friend and sometime lover. Together they pulled.

A fuffle under Dillon's shaggy coat made Sawyer open his eyes.

"Get off me, you mangy excuse for a rug!" Jerry struggled to squirm out from under Dillon's bulk. Dillon rolled and stayed on the floor. "I only like you on top when you've got two feet!"

"Bitch, bitch, bitch," Sawyer mocked the wolf, but he was on his feet in a flash. The alphas found each other in the shadows, but Sawyer wasn't sure he could find a beta wolf. "Get off your ass, you have work to do."

He yanked Jerry up, maybe a little more gently for recalling he'd been on his last breath not twenty seconds ago.

Brad knelt at Kevin's side, the baby in his arms squawking that wordless demand of *Do something, damn it!* "Don't die, please don't die, Kevin. I love you," the little fox keened. He might not have monogamy in him, but he had plenty of love for their cobbled-together family, Kevin most of all.

"Come on, Jerry." Sawyer wrapped his huge arms around the dying wolf and the healed one. "Remember how you had to seek Rudy!"

Jerry shut his eyes, his forehead wrinkled. "I can't find him, where... Brad, help us!"

Whatever the fox did, he used love and not strength. The moment Brad touched Kevin, a wolf-spark flared, bright enough to catch, hold, and drag into human.

"Shift, damn it!" Sawyer found a few leftover cuss words, but he could have saved his breath. Now he held not one but two naked young men, and had better get out of the way of the third.

Brad shoved the baby at Sawyer and dove into the pile. "You're okay, you're okay!" He sniffled in the wolves' arms, squirming and promising all the sex they could get it up for.

At last, Sawyer could hold his son. His perfect, longed-for, impossible-but-so real child. Who was wrinkly and slimy and screaming and the most beautiful thing in the world.

His darling was still wet, and getting chilly. Sawyer found a shirt on the floor that smelled of one of the enemy who wouldn't need it again. Wrapping the baby tenderly fixed one problem and suggested others—most of what Sawyer knew about babies involved poop.

The rest involved milk.

One problem he could solve, yay. Parking his squalling bundle between Dillon's furry paws, he knew he could rely on Papa Bear to mind the cub. Sawyer went to the kitchen, searching for things to improvise with. Yup, only took a minute! Milk from the walk-in fridge and gently warmed, a food service glove, and the tiniest of knife pricks, and he prepared cub's first dinner.

And something for Dillon. Twenty pounds of raw hamburger ought to do a bear good. The wolves could have the brats and hot dogs.

Seemed like forever since he'd burst through the doorway with blood in his eye, but really, only a few minutes. So much had changed, and their lives would never be the same.

Sawyer leaned against the furry bulk of his beloved bear, offering the little finger of his makeshift bottle to their cub. Little Boo-Boo latched on and his horrible cry gave way to a gurgle of contentment. He nestled in the curve of Sawyer's arm, sucking on the milk-filled glove.

Naked, bloody, surrounded by the enemy dead, leaning on the furry lover he'd come so desperately close to losing, and feeding the cub they'd brought forth, Sawyer had never been happier.

ᴢ

While little Boo-Boo nursed himself into a stupor, Kevin, Brad, and Jerry either ran or staggered to do some damage control. With Sawyer directing traffic, they locked doors and gathered up the slain wolves' personal effects. They might be rogues, but their families deserved to know the truth.

Brad came to watch the baby feed. "He's cute, but he's so... red."

He was, but a perfect color for a bear cub. Any color Boo-Boo was would be perfect for a bear cub—would his coat be tipped with silver when he shifted? Sawyer could be indulgent with Brad. "I think it passes."

Brad reached out to touch the baby's downy hair. "What are you naming him?"

Conscious of not yet consulting with Boo-Boo's other father, who currently communicated in grunts and coughs,
Sawyer hedged. "We haven't settled on the exact name." That
would be a conversation for later tonight, when Dillon came to
bed as a man, and they would make love and drowse, and talk
about the future they wanted for their child.

"What's your pick?" Brad gazed adoringly at the baby. So
did Sawyer. Of course. Such a perfect lil' guy.

"Something something Lawson Ballantine. Or maybe
Ballantine Lawson. We haven't decided." Sawyer never doubted they'd give their cub both their names, but he wouldn't assume. Urso he might be, but Dillon was his Arth and more im-
portantly, his mate and co-parent, and the one who'd carried
their cub in his body. When Dillon could talk again, they'd
discuss names. Maybe they'd discuss changing Dillon's name
to Ballantine too. Dillon groaned and turned under Sawyer,
curving around his family like a big hairy barricade. Sawyer
snuggled in tighter.

Sawyer could marvel at his cub all day, but he had business to tend to. "Bring my britches, Kevin," Sawyer requested.
"I need my phone."

He had so many calls to make: Rudy, to explain what
happened to his pack. Liza, to warn her of incoming, and
oh, dang, to have her get some diapers and whatever else
babies needed. Didn't have to be much, did it? He should
call Margo Frost, too: she'd kept Dillon alive through his
pregnancy in more ways than one. Sawyer owed her thanks,
and a few pointed questions about how she happened to
know so much. Oh hell, that was Rudy's job. Or Jerry's.
Sawyer would delegate.

And they'd need a truck from the job site to haul the seven

slain wolves up to the woods. They were pack: their bones could lie on Ballantine Mountain, but rogues deserved no honors.

Kevin had barely picked up Sawyer's trousers when twitters emerged from a pocket. He handed the phone over like it was a poisonous snake. An out of state call: Sawyer answered.

"Mr. Ballantine, I'm calling to see how Dillon's doing."

Sawyer glanced over his shoulder at Dillon, who was licking the last traces out of the hamburger wrapper. "Fine. Has a healthy appetite." All true, now. Explaining all the intermediate steps between fine human and fine bear, not happening. "I appreciate your checking on us, Dr. Livingston."

"I understand the concerns you expressed earlier, and I wanted you to know circumstances have changed."

They certainly had. "Did your receptionist have her baby? What about the other mother to be?" Sawyer inquired. Those were the only Possum Kingdom circumstances he knew of, and besides, he was awash in new-daddy joy. Everyone ought to have a baby! "How're they doing? How're the babies?" Obviously not one tenth as cute as Boo-Boo.

"Fine, fine, bless your heart for asking. Now, in the interests of keeping everyone fine, I've considered your request. I and the family can fly out any time, and I can keep an eye on Dillon until he's ready to deliver. We'll make sure you have a healthy baby, and erm, father."

Sawyer started to laugh, deep snorks fueled by irony and tinged with hysteria. Dillon twisted enough to lick Sawyer's thigh. Long swipes from a burger-y bear tongue didn't help. Sawyer laughed harder, his son bouncing on his chest. "Yes, of course. Come on out to Ballantine Mountain, Doc. Meet our cub."

CHAPTER TWENTY-ONE

A week after Dillon's homecoming, they rearranged the living room. The massive chairs and couches had been pushed to the perimeter of the cabin's living room. A fluffy white flokati rug lay in the clearing beneath the skylight. The sun angled in, bathing the white wool in a pool of warmth and light, making individual long strands glow.

Luscious smells wafted in from the maple and granite kitchen—Liza had outdone herself with creating a feast. Dillon was sure it would taste as good as it smelled, but his attempt to steal a nibble had been met with the thwap of a wooden spoon to his knuckles. Even the Arth of Ballantine Mountain obeyed the whims of the master chef.

Low voices drifted from down the hall, muttering while the speakers prepared for their roles. The clink of a belt buckle hitting the floor mixed with the thuds of shoes being toed off and the whisper of cotton sliding off muscled torsos.

Dillon followed the sounds.

Sawyer had already peeled down and was holding their child. Seven days old now, he now stayed awake a bit after his feedings. He was still in the hedgehog stage, and objected to being uncurled long enough to peel his one piece jammie suit off. Dillon couldn't resist tickling his sweet little tummy, now with an inny belly button. The cord falling away signaled the time for this gathering.

Dillon shrugged out of his own dress clothes, eyeing the way Sawyer held their son. Yes, he was Papa Bear, and no, that didn't keep Dillon from needing reassurance. "You might want to keep his diaper on until the very last minute."

"Probably." Sawyer smiled down into their cub's face. Dillon's heart nearly popped. No, he hadn't wanted this child, or hadn't known he wanted this child, until the little guy became a reality. But seeing the tiny being made of his beloved Sawyer and himself, he couldn't imagine how he'd ever doubted. He embraced his mate and their child. Sawyer met him with a kiss, sweet and chaste. It wouldn't do to display the depth of their bond right now, with a house full of guests.

"I'll save the rest for later." Dillon hated letting go of his family, but it was time.

Sawyer chuffed, loud enough to cut through the chatter. Silence fell.

He chuffed again, and Dillon chuffed with him.

The procession began until the leaders of all the shifter groups and their mates surrounded the white flokati. Maybe it wasn't the proper way, but Jerry, Kevin, and Brad were also part of the circle. They were family, they'd fought and come close to dying for this small bear cub. They'd earned the right to be there. And Brad could probably behave in a group of nude alphas. Oh good, he clasped his hands in front of his groin.

Dillon stripped Boo-Boo of his last wrapping and took Sawyer's arm.

Sawyer squeezed Dillon's hand between his upper arm and chest. "They speak once each, Dillon. Only once. Even Rudy."

With a deep breath, he nodded. Showtime.

Together they marched into the conclave of the alphas.

They took their position in front of the massive fireplace, between Rudy and the leader of the raccoons, and as one, they knelt at the edge of the flokati. Sawyer placed their cub in the center of the white fluff where the bright sun painted his skin. He wiggled at the tickly strands, and yawned a pink, toothless yawn.

Dillon and Sawyer rose, still linked. Dillon swung his gaze around the circle, finding pride in his friends' eyes, and open curiosity in others who weren't part of their social circle. Sawyer might be Urso of Ballantine Mountain and the leader of the united shifters, but many of the alphas never visited for the pleasure of their company. Mostly herbivores, imagine that.

Sawyer chuffed for attention again and began to speak. "Alphas, mates, friends. We present to you David Berend Lawson Ballantine, son and heir of Sawyer Ballantine, Urso of Ballantine Mountain, and Dillon Lawson, Arth of Ballantine Mountain."

Dillon tensed: half the guests were trying to have their say at the same time. Sawyer chuffed hard, bringing the guests to silence. "You may have your say. In an orderly fashion. Start at my right."

That made Rudy the first speaker. "The wolves of Ballantine Mountain welcome David, son of our friends Sawyer and Dillon." He turned stony eyes around the gathering, and Dillon himself might have thought twice about arguing.

Eric, Wapiti of the elk, stood at Rudy's right. Herbivore he might be, but fearsome in his own right. The elk shifters had given Dillon grief until Eric put a stop to the harassment some six months earlier. Sounded like Eric planned to put a stop to nonsense now. "The elk of Ballantine Mountain also welcome David, son of the Urso and Arth."

Liza gave a blessing on behalf of the bobcats, and the local possum Jack said something positive without falling over, though it looked a near thing. So far, so good.

Coyote, though, had to create a problem. "How is this the son of two men alone?"

The horrid question Dillon hoped wouldn't arise, but knew would be asked. His heart pounded: he wouldn't lie to the alphas, but neither would he explain. If they were limited to one speech apiece, he would limit himself the same. He forced his voice to ring out clearly. "I carried the child of my bonded mate, Sawyer Ballantine, in my body."

"Well how the hell did you do that?" Coyote demanded, but Dillon cut him off.

"You said your piece, Coyote." Would that be enough to end the comments?

"How the hell did you do that?" The Reynard of the foxes might have had his own question, but no, he would stick to the unwelcome theme.

"I don't understand exactly how, but I did, and here is our child." Dillon hadn't let go of Sawyer's arm, and only the contact gave him the strength to speak. He gripped harder: the next question would be—

"How did you, ah, get pregnant, if that's what we should call it?" That was the Puma, very sleek in his disdain.

"If you aren't clear on the mechanics of that, ask your wife to explain," Sawyer answered smoothly. A titter went up around the circle.

The Puma went red, and he examined his fingernails instead of looking at the assembly, or thank goodness, at Dillon.

Just like a cat, cover his embarrassment with grooming. Dillon restrained a smile.

"Assuming we can guess at how this little fellow started, though really we can't, because really now, you're a man and all, but all the same we think we should..." wittered the Stag of the mule deer. The presence of the Puma at his side seemed to make him nervous. Or maybe he was always twitchy.

Wait, what was Dillon supposed to answer? The Stag sort of asked a question, but hadn't really—

"Next," Sawyer directed.

Moon, shine on this wonderful bear for chopping that off. No wonder Dillon loved the big lug.

"Tell us about the birth." Otter had his ducks in a row, damn it.

Just thinking about being torn open and his cub ripped away made Dillon both ill and furious, and turned his voice to a snarl. "I had an inadvertent C-section, courtesy of some rogue wolves." He swung around to show the assembly the remaining scars on his belly, deep tracks where Brian and the pack had torn him open.

"Can any of them bear witness to this?" was Beaver's question.

"This is my mate," Sawyer growled. "Surely you jest."

Funny, the few who remained to speak didn't ask any more rude questions.

"Sniff and know him," Sawyer commanded. "This is David, son of Sawyer and Dillon."

If he wasn't a shifter himself, and bigger and badder than anyone here except his mate, Dillon might have shat himself at the collection of wildlife materializing in his living room. He might anyway, all those fangs and claws and hooves near his child. All those noses. Smarking on his cub. Snorfling at him. All too easy to take a bite... He'd nearly died to keep wolves from biting, and he would again, if he had to spatter every wall in the cabin with their guests.

"Easy, Dillon," Sawyer whispered, but his arm went rock hard with the tension. "Easy."

But Dillon could only relax a fraction when each alpha returned to two-legged form and pronounced themselves satisfied.

Dillon growled when the Puma came back for another sniff. Damned cat was gonna get ripped limb from limb. Gonna get his tail pulled at the very least. Gonna... Dillon tensed to snatch the lord of the cougars away from his child. Quit sniffing!

A roar of laughter went up before Dillon got both hands on that thrashing tail. Puma jerked back, his ears flat to his head and whiskers plastered to his cheeks. He dripped.

"Fountain Boy's got some water pressure to him, don't he?" Rudy drawled.

⚡

At last the party ended, without bloodshed, without more questions, and with everyone clothed again—fur was fine, but so were party togs. Everyone asked all they were entitled to in the ceremony. Dillon growled the conversational snooping into oblivion. He was Arth of Ballantine Mountain, and not to be pried at. Gossip couldn't be helped, and they'd have some choice comments for a man who produced a living child and had his flat, if scarred, belly. Anyone who wanted another look at Davie had to come to either him, or Sawyer, because Liza tended to snarl when anyone got too close while she held the baby. Their son had a fearsome granny.

Davie slept through most of the excitement.

The few guests who were staying swirled off to find their bedrooms. In the morning Sawyer would send Rudy down the mountain alone to run the job site, now festooned with the correct green electrical cable and starting to sprout drywall. In the meantime, he and his lover Eric would likely miss the playroom, and hopefully manage to find their way back to their own bedroom before getting too friendly.

Jerry, Kevin, and Brad tugged Troy down the hall to their usual room: Dillon was beyond grateful the elk hadn't been involved in the fracas that resulted in his son's birth. Troy'd been very helpful passing canapés tonight though.

"Come. I want to show you something." Sawyer motioned toward a door down the hall, usually kept closed.

Dillon quirked a brow and held Davie closer. "The playroom?"

"Come and see." One side of Sawyer's mouth lifted, but he shuffled a bit from one foot to the other, so unlike his normal alpha, take-no-prisoners self. He opened the door and stepped aside.

Dillon winced and stepped inside. Instead of a dreary, dark place, he found light and nary a reminder of the room's former purpose.

"Wow! So this is what you've been up to, what you wouldn't let me see!" Of course, he couldn't help noticing a new door in the wall of their bedroom. Dillon held Davie and spun around in the space where a sling once stood. Now, instead of sporting whips and toys, the walls were covered with murals of the mountains. Liza, in bobcat form, peeked out from underneath a bush, and the more he inspected the painting, the more creatures he found familiar.

"This way, all his nearest and dearest will be keeping an eye on him." Sawyer gave him a somewhat sheepish smile. "I...I hope you like it."

"Like it? I love it!" He ran a loving hand over the smooth wood of the crib. "You made this yourself?"

"Every piece." A flare of pride rode a wave of energy, a nearly tangible thing.

All the time Dillon spent sulking, Sawyer spent creating the perfect place for their son to grow and begin to explore his world.

"Yes, I love it." He crossed the distance to his mate. "And I love you." He nuzzled noses with his mate until the new boss of the house let loose a wail.

Sawyer sighed. "Hold that thought."

Dillon retired to the master bedroom with Davie and a bottle. He cradled his child, smiling at the way his little pursed lips worked against the nipple. So this was contentment.

Sawyer squished into the big chair with them, wrapping an arm over Dillon's shoulders. He leaned his head against Dillon's to help him watch their cub feed. No, *this* was contentment.

At last Davie drifted off, his lips still twitching now and then for a last drop of milk. Sawyer scrambled out of the chair first and lifted the tiny sleeper. He pressed a kiss to Davie's forehead that made Dillon's heart go pitty-pat. His big growly bear, all turned to mush by their son. Sawyer lay the sleeping baby in his bassinet next to the big bed.

"You did remind Brad he can't jump in to snuggle until Davie graduates to the crib?" Sawyer whispered.

"Very firmly." Dillon had wakened to the sight of a bushy red plume hanging out of the bassinet this morning. He'd yanked the tail like a door-pull.

"Good. Now, since our cub is asleep, I suggest we have a little, ah, grownup time." Sawyer's smile went from baby-besotted to lascivious. He put his arms out for Dillon to step into.

How had he done without the joy of his mate? All those weeks alone with his anger and his fear? When Sawyer wanted nothing more than to be joyous about the little Boo-Boo who now had a real name.

Dillon plastered himself belly to belly with Sawyer, wrapping his big bear in his arms. There'd be kisses if he would only tip his face. "Sawyer, I have to tell you something first."

Sawyer loosened his embrace enough that Dillon had room to step back. "Oh? What?" His voice had a tinge of fear.

"I have to tell you I'm sorry. I was scared and angry about getting pregnant, and I still think it's the weirdest thing to ever happen to me, but... I shouldn't have taken it out on you. I should have stayed, and we should have talked, and..." Dillon ran out of words. "I made you miss our son growing, and if I wasn't insisting on being alone, we could have gotten him born some safer way. So, I'm sorry."

Sawyer pulled him close again, and buried his face in Dillon's neck for a moment. A tremor ran through his frame, and he pulled back to look Dillon in the eye. "I'm sorry too. I made a lot of unwarranted assumptions. That was unworthy of me."

"You'll make it up to me by minding Davie while I'm studying for finals." Dillon would find the energy to finish what he'd started, because neither Sawyer's business nor his own were going away. Although if he slung Davie across his chest, he could still read his notes....

"I will, and you'll ace your classes. Have to set a good example for our cub." Sawyer's smile went lopsided. "All I could think about was the miracle we'd been given, and I didn't consider what it was like for you. How scary it must have been, and it was all my fault."

"You can't say I didn't help." Dillon squeezed hard. "Boo-Boo, well, Davie, definitely took both of us. I think he kind of looks like you."

"Doesn't he mostly look like other babies right now?" Sawyer glanced into the bassinet. "He's not red anymore."

That got Sawyer a ringing swat to the backside. "I say he looks like his daddy. Argue with Papa Bear at your own risk."

Dillon followed the swat with a bit of glute-groping. Damn, Sawyer had a nice ass. And he hadn't had a good handful of that delectable rump in weeks—between the pregnancy and his fury, recovering from the pregnancy and from the horrific mauling he'd taken, not to mention jumping out of a sound sleep every two hours when Boo-Boo cried. He hadn't managed to stay awake long enough to take advantage. Sawyer had gathered him up into a massive bear-pile and let him sleep, safe and warm, every time they'd gotten near a bed.

"Who'd arguing with Papa Bear now?" Sawyer swatted back. Funny, he seemed to have the same kind of hunger for Dillon's butt—he squeezed both sides.

Their cocks rose, making fat logs inside the dress slacks that had become entirely too confining. Just rubbing against Sawyer's erection felt nice, but Dillon wanted more than nice, he wanted skin touching skin. Start with untucking his big bear's shirt, and stuffing his hands down the back of his slacks. Oh, warm, with a slight scratch of body hair... Dillon needed to get them stripped as fast as he could.

Might have gone too fast—he thought he'd wear that shirt again someday, but Liza might be able to sew the buttons back on. Who cared anyway—the silly thing kept him from being naked with his mate.

Sawyer never lost his lip lock as he bore them backwards toward the bed. Dillon let Sawyer guide him—safely past the bassinet—and onto his back. With his beloved's weight upon him, Dillon strove to thrust his tongue into Sawyer's mouth. Oh Moon, he'd missed the sheer brawling romp of sex.

With Sawyer. He needed his mate in a bone-deep way, needed to know they were good with each other again, could rebuild their cracked love into something fire-forged and strong.

The fire grew hotter—Sawyer fastened his mouth at the side of Dillon's neck, flicking his tongue against the big strap muscle. Dillon writhed, not so far as to actually make Sawyer stop. "That's intense!"

"Mmm hmm," Sawyer agreed, lashing his tongue against Dillon's neck. "Mmm."

Yeah, mmm. Seemed to be a straight circuit from his neck to his cock. Dillon gasped when Sawyer started to suck. "That's gonna make a hickey."

"Mmm hmm." His smile sounded clearly. And Sawyer was enjoying himself. So was Dillon. He'd wear the love bite like a trophy, because yeah...

Leaving off Dillon's neck, Sawyer worshipped his way down Dillon's body. Across his collarbones, down his breastbone, across his mounded pecs. Kissing and laving his way through the light coating of hair covering his chest. Dillon ran his hands through Sawyer's hair, a glossy dark pelt now, each strand very soft and dear.

Sawyer moved lower, finding ridges of abs now. And the furrows of his scars. Would Sawyer—?

"You don't have to lick those." Dillon curled upward, ready to push Sawyer away. Not away, just down. Or up. Or over. Just—not. Not there.

"They're part of you." Sawyer left off kissing to gaze upwards with eyes gone dark. "I love all parts of you."

"I know, but..." Dillon faltered. "I mean, I'm glad, but..."

"Do they hurt?" Sawyer asked.

"No. Not now. But... They aren't pretty." Not like he'd been, with a buff, unmarked body. Now he looked like he'd come through a war. He had, but Sawyer didn't have to...

Apparently Sawyer did. With gentle strokes he ran his tongue through the valleys and kissed the punctures, red and hairless still. "These are marks of honor." He paused in his tracing. "They make you more dear to me, because of how and why you gained them."

He sounded so sincere—Dillon wanted to believe him. For a moment, he could, did. And then Sawyer stopped his exploring and lay his head against Dillon's belly. Had he said what he truly believed, deep down? Or did he merely utter words he thought Dillon wanted to hear?

"The scars should be on me." Sawyer's breath riffled the fine hairs on Dillon's belly. "You got them because I failed you. I swore I'd let nothing bad happen to you, and I failed you. I'm sorry I didn't get there sooner."

"You got there in time." Would his scars be a constant reminder to Sawyer of a promise he couldn't keep? Should Dillon shift right now? Every time he did he came back a little more whole. "I'll keep trying to fade them, I promise."

"You don't have to." Sawyer rubbed his cheek against Dillon's belly. "You are beautiful to me in all ways. And besides..." He caught Dillon's hand, bringing the fingers to his face to trace the white scar across his cheek. Sawyer'd been slashed to the bone when he'd slain the rogues who'd killed his family and his sleuth. "You've never said anything about this."

Dillon cupped his hand against Sawyer's cheek, appalled. "Why would I? That's a battle scar."

"Exactly." Sawyer turned to lay a kiss on Dillon's palm, and another on his belly, in a tender furrow. "So are these."

They were. And now Dillon could trust his words. "I love you, Sawyer."

Nobody who wasn't a bear would believe how fast Sawyer could move. In a heartbeat he was full length against Dillon again, mouth to mouth. Their noses bumped and it didn't matter, only that their lips found home, their tongues darting and licking. Nothing mattered, except Sawyer's furry hide plastered to Dillon's, and that he hugged as ardently as Dillon clutched him.

"I love you too." Sawyer came up for air. "I love you so much."

Nothing mattered more right now than getting Sawyer's cock into him. Dillon spared an arm for groping at the bedside table. They had lube, plus the other necessary. "Um..."

"Yes, we'll use a condom." Sawyer untangled enough to reach into the drawer. He found a big box Dillon didn't think they'd had during hibernation. They certainly hadn't used such things. And now Davie made living proof of the lack.

Thank Moon Sawyer was on the same wavelength. Dillon ripped open the packet and smoothed the squishy latex over his mate's throbbing cock. Sawyer's cock lifted with each beat of his heart, jumping under Dillon's hands. Silly extra step, no wonder they'd stopped using rubbers the minute they thought they could.

Hah on that. Suppose he ought to learn how to roll one down with his lips.

"Lube me, big bear." Dillon lifted his knees, exposing himself to his lover. Sawyer's thick fingers breached his hole. How had he gone so long without Sawyer's touch? Well, yeah, but... Dillon gave himself over to the familiar stretch.

Oh how he'd missed the thrill of his beloved mate pushing in. Joining with him. Entering him. Dillon wrapped his legs around Sawyer's butt and pulled him closer. "Come on in."

Damn but he loved the way Sawyer's eyes fluttered shut, and then opened again, to gaze directly into Dillon's face. "Nowhere I'd rather be."

Moving together. Loving each other. Holding Sawyer tight and feeling the heft of his lover's muscular body. Slow. Intense.

And all Dillon ever wanted.

He'd been a fool.

And might be again.

Because Davie needed a sister.

About the Authors

You will know Eden Winters by her distinctive white plumage and exuberant cry of "Hey, y'all!" in a Southern US drawl so thick it renders even the simplest of words unrecognizable. Watch out, she hugs!

She's trudged down hallways with police detectives, learned to disarm knife-wielding bad guys, and witnessed the correct way to blow doors off buildings. Her e-mail contains various snippets of forensic wisdom, such as "What would a dead body left in a Mexican drug tunnel look like after six months?" In the process of her adventures she has written fourteen m/m romance novels, has won several Rainbow Awards, was a Lambda Awards Finalist, and lives in terror of authorities showing up at her door to question her Internet searches. When not putting characters in dangerous situations she's a mild-mannered business executive, mother, grandmother, vegetarian, and PFLAG activist.

Her natural habitats are airports, coffee shops, and on the backs of motorcycles.

P.D. Singer lives in Colorado with her slightly bemused husband, one proto-adult, and Old Man Cat. She's a big believer in research, first-hand if possible, so the reader can be quite certain Pam has skied down a mountain face-first, been stepped on by rodeo horses, acquired a potato burn or two, and will never, ever, write a novel that includes sky-diving.

When not writing, playing her fiddle, or skiing, she can be found with a book in hand.

More shifters from Eden Winters and P.D. Singer

 Meet Sawyer, Dillon, Brad, and the other shifters of Ballantine Mountain in their first sexy adventure.

 When otter shifter Lon meets Corey on the slopes, they're in for some good times in the mountains. Until the werewolves show up.

 Dr. Dusty Livingston has a passel of cranky possums who need a leader: can whoops-I'm-a-shifter? Seth step up to the pump?